St Elizab

Dealing with ... ...artbreaking,
funny, and ... ...g, often all at once!

This series takes a look at a hospital set up
especially to deal with such children,
peeping behind the scenes into almost all the
departments and clinics, exploring the
problems and solutions of various diseases,
while watching the staff fall helplessly
in love—with the kids and with each other.

Enjoy!

Margaret O'Neill started scribbling at four and began nursing at twenty. She contracted TB and, when recovered, did her British Tuberculosis Association nursing training before general training at the Royal Portsmouth Hospital. She married, had two children, and, with her late husband, she owned and managed several nursing homes. Now retired and living in Sussex, she still has many nursing contacts. Her husband would have been delighted to see her books in print.

Recent titles by the same author:

Cottage Hospital
A Question of Honour
Doctor on Skye
In Safe Hands
Seeds of Love
Handful of Dreams
Christmas is Forever
*Never Past Loving**
*Long Hot Summer**
*Take a Deep Breath**
*No Longer a Stranger**
Downland Clinic
The Generous Heart
More Than Skin Deep
A Cautious Loving
Double Trouble
The Practice Wife
The Patient Man

*Linked quartet

THE GUARDIAN HEART

MARGARET O'NEILL

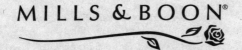
MILLS & BOON®

DID YOU PURCHASE THIS BOOK WITHOUT A COVER?

If you did, you should be aware it is **stolen property** as it was reported *unsold and destroyed* by a retailer. Neither the author nor the publisher has received any payment for this book.

All the characters in this book have no existence outside the imagination of the author, and have no relation whatsoever to anyone bearing the same name or names. They are not even distantly inspired by any individual known or unknown to the author, and all the incidents are pure invention.

All Rights Reserved including the right of reproduction in whole or in part in any form. This edition is published by arrangement with Harlequin Enterprises II B.V. The text of this publication or any part thereof may not be reproduced or transmitted in any form or by any means, electronic or mechanical, including photocopying, recording, storage in an information retrieval system, or otherwise, without the written permission of the publisher.

This book is sold subject to the condition that it shall not, by way of trade or otherwise, be lent, resold, hired out or otherwise circulated without the prior consent of the publisher in any form of binding or cover other than that in which it is published and without a similar condition including this condition being imposed on the subsequent purchaser.

MILLS & BOON and MILLS & BOON with the Rose Device are registered trademarks of the publisher.

First published in Great Britain 2000
Harlequin Mills & Boon Limited,
Eton House, 18-24 Paradise Road, Richmond, Surrey TW9 1SR

© Margaret O'Neill 2000

ISBN 0 263 82434 9

Set in Times Roman 10½ on 12 pt.
112-0011-51700

Printed and bound in Spain
by Litografia Rosés S.A., Barcelona

CHAPTER ONE

THREE days after Holly joined the élite staff of St Elizabeth's Children's Hospital, Ben Harvey invited her out for a drink.

At least, Holly interpreted it as a drink; his actual words were, 'What about joining me for a night of wine and romance, Staff Nurse Holly Brown?' He glanced sideways at her, his brilliant hazel-green eyes sparkling as they walked side by side down the ward.

Nice voice, she thought—husky, full of laughter.

Warning bells clanged in Holly's mind. 'Beware Ben Harvey, our registrar with the roving eye,' Jan Howard, one of the other senior staff nurses on General Medical, had warned her on her first morning. Adding with a laugh, 'Mind you, if I weren't already saddled with a jealous husband and a couple of kids, I wouldn't say no to a night out with Ben. He's a poppet, an antidote to a grey winter's day.'

'So why the warning?' Holly had asked.

'If you're looking for anything long term, forget it. He's a confirmed bachelor, thirty-something, and in between dating all and sundry is working for his fellowship and a consultancy. He's a fast mover and very bright with it. You can't fault him as a doctor, but as a man—watch out.'

Holly, having just witnessed his gentle, thorough examination of three-year-old little Cindy Marsh, who had been admitted suffering from pyrexia of unknown origin, couldn't fault him. Meningitis had been ruled out, thank God, but there were a dozen other nasty conditions that might be present.

Cindy's mother had been nervous, and little Cindy with her high, fluctuating temperature, had been fractious and tearful. Somehow Ben had reassured them both. He had actually made Cindy giggle when he'd carefully pulpated her tiny rigid abdomen, and had got her to blow on his stethoscope to warm it before sounding her skinny chest.

'We'll keep Cindy in for a few days,' he explained to Mrs Marsh, his voice gentle, 'make her more comfortable and see how things go. It is quite possible that this temperature will go away of its own accord and she will be back to normal. Any experienced mum will tell you that this sort of thing happens with children, nobody knows why.' He shot Holly a smile across the bed. 'I'm sure Nurse Holly will confirm that, won't you, Nurse?'

Holly nodded. 'Sure will,' she said cheerfully, taking her cue from Ben. 'Kids can be up one minute and down the next and they have this amazing ability to bounce back.'

Ben laid his hand on the young mother's shoulder. 'Silly thing to say, but try not to worry, Mrs Marsh. We'll take good care of Cindy, and if there is an underlying cause for this fluctuating temperature, we'll suss it out.' He stroked the little girl's hot forehead. 'I want you to drink a lot for me, Cindy—will you do that, please? Milk, water, fizzy drinks, anything you fancy.'

The child looked up at him, eyes febrile bright in her flushed face. 'Yes,' she whispered.

So that was Ben the doctor, thought Holly as they walked away from the bed a few minutes later, and this is Ben the man inviting me out for a drink or whatever he calls it. Just as Jan said, there's a hell of a difference between lightweight man and dedicated doctor—what a package. I rather think I like it, and if he's footloose and fancy-free, well, so am I.

They reached the nurses' station halfway down the ward. There wasn't a nurse in sight.

Ben was grinning down at her. It was a wide, infectious grin revealing even white teeth, except for a chip at the corner of the central incisor. 'I can see the wheels churning,' he said, 'so what's the verdict? Will you risk your reputation and let me wine you and dine you? I promise, no strings attached.'

Holly found herself grinning back up at him. 'I haven't had time to establish a reputation as yet,' she said, 'so I've nothing to risk, provided that you mean it about there being no strings. I definitely am not into anything heavy, but neither—'

'Are you into one-night stands,' he interrupted.

'Exactly.' She opened little Cindy's case notes as she saw Bob Roper, the most senior staff nurse, approaching.

Ben bent over the notes with her. Their two heads were almost touching and she could feel the heat from his cheek.

'Like the perfume,' he murmured.

'Like yours,' she retorted, catching a wisp of lemony aftershave.

He chuckled. '*Touché!* Put on something cool and stunning and I'll pick you up at eight in Reception.'

'You look like the cat that's had the cream,' pronounced Jan Howard, when she came on duty at five to relieve

Holly. 'Come on, give—what's put that ear-to-ear smile on your face?'

Holly said lightly, 'I'm simply by nature happy and optimistic.'

'And then some.' Jan tilted her head to one side and eyed Holly carefully. 'You've got a date,' she surmised. 'And since you've been on duty since seven this morning, it's got to be someone on the staff. You might as well come clean, it'll be all over Lizzie's by nightfall—our grapevine's second to none.'

'I could have had a phone call or letter.'

'But I bet a month's salary that you haven't.' Her eyes widened suddenly. 'It's with our roving registrar,' she squeaked. 'He's the only guy around who can light up a girl the way you're all lit up.'

Holly dimpled. 'I give up—yep, it's with Ben Harvey.'

'In spite of my warning,' said Jan, trying to sound severe.

'In spite of that. Actually, it suits me fine. Like Ben, I'm not looking for anything heavy—light and frothy is what I'm after.'

'Well, that's Ben's style.' Jan raised an imaginary glass. 'Here's to a bright, breezy, short-lived relationship. Go out tonight and enjoy.'

'Cool and stunning,' Holly murmured out loud as she searched through her wardrobe for something that would fit the bill. Re-hitching the towel that she'd wrapped herself in after she'd showered, she zipped the hangers along the rail and flung three possibles onto the bed.

There must be something that would match up to Ben's sophisticated tastes—at least, from his reputation she supposed they were sophisticated. OK, so even the smartest of Shropshire stores might not stock a selection to match Harrods, and even if they had she couldn't have afforded designer models on the junior staff nurse's salary she'd been earning in her previous job. In fact she had done most of her shopping in Maggie's in the arcade—not exactly an up-market boutique, but classy of its kind.

Out of the three outfits on the bed, she selected a sapphire-blue silky slip of a dress that matched her eyes. Well, it was cool, she decided. Stunning—she wasn't sure; perhaps she was a bit too rounded for the clinging silk. A young houseman she had dated had once described her as being 'small and cuddly'.

She let the towel slip and eyed herself critically in the wardrobe mirror. She wasn't fat, but neither did she look as if she were bordering on being anorexic. Her waist was slender enough, so were her hips, but her breasts certainly didn't comply with the fashionable non-existent look— they were softly rounded and tilted pertly upwards.

'Oh, well, what you can't change you must learn to live with, as Granny would say,' she muttered. 'But you're not in too bad shape for twenty-six.'

The dress in fact looked pretty good, she decided a few minutes later, smoothing it down over her lacy bra and wispy panties. She pulled on dark blue sheer silk stockings and wiggled her feet into strappy black sandals; brushed her cap of crisp tawny hair till it gleamed; touched her lips with rose-red lipstick; sprayed herself liberally with her favourite perfume, and knew herself to be as ready as she ever would be.

What to wear topwise? It wasn't raining, but it was blowy—not the night for the flimsy wrap she fancied. It would have to be her trusty old black velvet jacket. At least it contrasted nicely with the blue. She slung it casually round her shoulders. 'Here's hoping that I meet your specifications, Ben, and pass for cool and stunning,' she muttered as she let herself out of her flat.

That she did was quite evident by the appreciative sparkle in Ben's eyes when he met her in the foyer.

'Fab-u-lous,' he drawled as he came towards her, hands outstretched. 'Love the dress, matches your eyes to perfection.' He drew her hands up to his lips and kissed her knuckles.

Holly felt the blood rush into her cheeks and pulled her hands from his. 'Fool,' she muttered, smiling abstractedly at some of the people milling around nearby.

Ben chuckled; he had a lovely rich chuckle. 'You'll have to forgive my Latin ways,' he said, taking her elbow and steering her past the shopping mall along the spacious, glassed in, conservatory-like entry. 'I have some Italian in me three generations back, a great-grand-mother—very demonstrative, Italians.'

Holly, almost running to keep up with his long strides, said breathlessly, 'What, with your hair and eyes?'

He pulled a face. 'It's true, I missed out on the dark Latin good looks and inherited my handsome physiognomy from my Celtic ancestors.'

The automatic entrance doors opened and a shaft of cold air greeted them. Holly slipped her arms into the sleeves of her jacket.

Ben peered out into the well-lit asphalted area. There was a taxi waiting at the kerb. The driver hooted. 'Ours, I think,' he said, whisking her across the pavement.

The Greenhouse lived up to its name. There were shrubs, potted plants and mini palm trees everywhere. Small tables for two, covered with brightly coloured check cloths, were tucked away, each in their own little arbour of greenery. The lighting was a discreet orange glow, supplemented by the light from the candles in low, old-fashioned candle holders at the centre of each table. And over everything the mouth watering aroma of well-cooked food.

'This is quite something,' breathed Holly, when the waiter had gone away, leaving them to wade through their menus. 'I have never seen a restaurant like this before…' she dimpled a smile across at Ben '…but then I suppose that simply proves that I'm an innocent just arrived in the big, wicked city.'

Ben looked straight into her eyes, his were twinkling. 'Your eyes,' he murmured, 'really are blue as sapphires— or is it gentians? And, for what it's worth, I don't buy the innocent bit.'

Deliberately provocative, Holly fluttered her long lashes, Unmascaraed, they were a little darker than her tawny hair. 'In the ways of the big city I am. Except for touching down at Heathrow, I've only been to London a couple of times before. Once on a school trip visiting museums and galleries, an educational package…'

'And the other?'

'You don't want to know,' she said. 'Boring stuff.'

'But I do, I want to know all about you, Holly Brown.'

Did he? Why, if theirs was to be a fun relationship? His elbows were on the table and he was resting his chin on his linked fingers, his brilliant hazel-green eyes inches from her own.

'Really! For a no-strings-attached evening out?'

'For the foundation of a future friendly easy relationship.'

Holly thought for a moment. He sounded sincere. 'OK, I'll fill you in on my background if you do the same.'

His eyebrows shot up. He looked startled. 'Do you really want to know about me?'

'As much as you want to know about me, otherwise…'

He grinned. 'I'll have an unfair advantage.'

What a nice mouth he's got, she thought, grinning back at him, and how quickly he catches onto what I'm thinking. 'Precisely.'

Ben stared into the beautiful, intelligent blue eyes, and discovered to his surprise that he really did want to get to know this stunning girl better—it wasn't just an opening gambit. 'You're a hard woman, Holly Brown,' he said.

'As granite,' she retorted dryly. 'You go first.'

'Not a lot to tell.' He shrugged. 'I've always lived and worked in London, I'm a city boy born and bred.'

Holly shuddered. 'Don't you ever want to get away from London? I couldn't bear it if I thought that I wouldn't be able to go back to Shropshire from time to time for a bit of peace and quiet, and to breathe some fresh air. I'm sure I'm going to like it here, and work's brilliant, but…'

'It's a far cry from the wide open countryside and you're homesick, aren't you?'

'I think perhaps I am,' she murmured, 'just a weeny bit. Silly, isn't it?'

He shook his head, finding her simple, unaffected honesty appealing.

'No, not silly. Have you been to Regent's Park yet? It's only a stone's throw from Lizzie's, and, believe it or not, there's plenty of oxygen to inhale there. Don't condemn us till you've sampled our London parks, Holly, they really are the lungs of the city. And they can be quiet too.

Stand in the centre of a large park, early morning or late evening, and you can hardly hear the traffic.'

Holly smiled. 'My word, you are passionate in defence of your home patch, aren't you? And, no, I haven't been to Regent's Park or anywhere for that matter. I only arrived here a few days ago and I'm still orientating myself round the hospital. With the shopping mall and all the facilities, it's a bit like a small town in itself. St Columbus was sizeable, but nothing to match Lizzie's.'

The waiter returned to take their order.

Holly took a glance at her menu and murmured apologetically, 'Oh, I haven't...'

'Shall I come back, sir?' asked the waiter.

Ben shook his head. 'No, we won't be a minute. Holly, will you let me order for you?'

'Please.'

'Are you on a diet? Is there anything you dislike?'

'I don't eat veal, otherwise...' She spread her hands eloquently.

'Nor I,' said Ben, inordinately pleased that they had this small moral code in common. 'They specialise here in well-cooked English, or perhaps I should say British, food. So how about smoked Scottish salmon for starters, followed by pork chops with masses of vegetables?'

Her eyes sparkled. 'Sounds marvellous. I should diet, but I do like my food—comes from growing up on a farm, I suppose.'

'Don't ever think of dieting,' Ben growled, when the waiter had gone. 'You're just right as you are, and a woman who isn't a slave to calories—makes you unique.'

The wine waiter arrived.

'And this,' explained Ben, 'is where we leave behind all things British, and sample something from The

Greenhouse's extensive international wine cellar. May I suggest something light, white and dry—unless you would prefer sweet?'

'I like dry,' said Holly. She didn't really care what they drank, although she knew that she had quite a good palate for wine. But it didn't matter tonight. She felt bubbly enough without wine. She watched Ben as he went into a huddle with the waiter. There was a definite hint of red in his chestnut hair—his Celtic origins? But his eloquent hand movements were all Italian. A heady mixture!

The rest of the evening flashed past. They talked non stop in between eating and drinking. Books, the state of the world, environmental issues, global warming, their small patients, their medical and nursing colleagues, and a little about themselves. The chipped tooth, she learned, was an old rugby trophy.

'And no way am I going to have it repaired,' Ben said vehemently. 'It was honourably earned on the field of battle, evidence of one of my finest tries.' He pulled a rueful face. 'Sorry, tend to go on a bit about rugby—mustn't bore you.'

'You're not,' Holly assured him. 'My three brothers play, and I've been going to matches since I could recognise that the best balls are oval, not round.' She gave a little chuckly laugh. 'Do you still play?'

'Only occasionally these days for hospital charity matches.' He beamed his nice wide smile across at her. 'You must come when I next play.'

'I should like that.'

To their mutual delight, they found that they had much more in common than just rugby—dancing, for instance.

'We'll go dancing one evening,' promised Ben. 'I know a nice little club where they do old and new stuff.' His mouth curved into a wide smile. 'We'll put on our glad rags and dance the night away,' he added, dropping a kiss on her cheek as he bid her goodnight at the door of the staff residency. 'See you in the morning, when you're all crisp and neat, and efficiently doing your Florence Nightingale bit.' Then, after kissing her on her other cheek, he strode away without a backward glance.

For a few moments Holly watched his broad back as he marched along the well-lit path connecting the residency with the hospital, then punched in the security code and let herself into the block of flats.

Once in bed, she meant to lie awake and mull over the events of the evening and relive them, but the moment her head touched the pillow she fell asleep.

A few miles away across the city, Ben was lying in bed unable to sleep, his head full of sapphire-blue eyes and a chuckly voice. He was amazed at how much he had enjoyed the evening. He had taken a bit of a chance inviting out someone as new to Lizzie's as Holly. As a rule, he held back until he knew a little about those he fancied, till he was reasonably sure of their expectations.

Occasionally caution misfired, but generally speaking his partings with a succession of girlfriends had been amicable because they'd started off without any unfillable promises.

Yet he had found himself inviting Holly out after meeting her for the first time that morning—and he didn't regret it for an instant. But what instinct had made him plump for The Greenhouse instead of a more trendy restaurant to dine?

It hadn't been what he'd originally intended. That had been a nightclub with loud music, where they charged the earth for inferior champagne and a lettuce leaf and half a tomato, and talking was almost impossible. Yet without exchanging more than a few words with Holly, and in spite of her bright and breezy manner, he had known that she would appreciate good food and good conversation.

It had been a risk; he might have been wildly wrong; it might have turned out to be dull—but it hadn't. In fact he hadn't been so intrigued by a woman for yonks.

'I can't wait to get to know you better, Staff Nurse Holly Brown,' he murmured into the darkness. His last thought, before dropping into a deep and dreamless sleep, was that he would see Holly in the morning.

The following morning, Holly stood just inside the ward door looking down the long central aisle. She listened to the babble of children's voices coming from the ten small wards opening off on either side, and felt a warm glow of pride and happiness steal over her. She let out a little contented sigh. The euphoria was still there a few weeks after her interview when she had learned that she had been accepted onto the staff of St Elizabeth's, the celebrated children's hospital.

Other hospitals might be crying out for staff, but it was a challenge to get into 'Lizzie's' as it was affectionately known.

'We only employ the *crème de la crème*,' Mrs Imogen Drew, the principal nursing officer, had told Holly at her interview. 'All our nursing staff are registered, except for students doing their try-out experience. They never work alone, always under the supervision of trained staff, and part of your job is to teach and supervise. A lot of nurses are good at hands-on stuff, but are not very good teachers. Will you be able to cope with teaching, Miss Brown?'

'Certainly,' Holly had replied confidently. 'I enjoyed teaching at my last hospital where I did my first specialist staffing on the paediatric ward. We had lots of students doing their course at the nearby university, and spending a few weeks on each ward to see which branch of nursing they wanted to opt for. Many of them were interested in children's nursing.'

Mrs Drew looked down at Holly's CV. 'That was at St Columbus, a general hospital in Shropshire,' she said. 'It's certainly got a splendid reputation.'

'The best,' replied Holly enthusiastically. 'And I loved working there, but I wanted to work in a hospital dedicated to children, and when this post came up at St Elizabeth's…' She spread her hands expressively.

'There was no contest.' Mrs Drew smiled, obviously pleased with Holly's explanation. For a moment she had looked thoughtfully at Holly, then stretched a hand out across the desk. 'Welcome aboard for a trial run, Miss Brown. You'll be hearing from Personnel about a contract—initially a short-term one, but with a longer one to follow if we suit each other.'

The interview had been in January, and now, at the end of March, she had started her probationary period as a senior staff nurse on General Medicine, and was enjoying every minute of it.

A small boy in a wheelchair came whizzing down the aisle towards her, skilfully avoiding the scattering of toys littering the floor and weaving round a cleaner wielding an outsize vacuum cleaner. 'Look out, Nurse Holly,' he shouted as he drew near.

Laughing, Holly skipped briskly to one side as he approached. 'Do you mind, Billy Bowman? This isn't Brands Hatch,' she said, trying to sound severe. 'One day, my lad, you're going to run somebody down and you'll have Sister Millett after you.'

'No way.' Billy shook his head, his chubby face alight with laughter beneath his bristly scrub of ginger hair. 'Sister Birdy knows that I won't run anybody over. I'm good, I am. See!' He spun the chair round on its rear wheels several times and then took off back down the ward.

He's right, thought Holly, staring after him, admiring the way he manipulated his wheelchair like the veteran that he was. He's brilliant with that chair. He had been wheelchair bound for the last three years since he was five, when he'd developed a brain tumour causing pressure on the spinal cord. The tumour had been successfully removed, but not before it had caused paralysis of his legs. He had spent so much time in Lizzie's over the years that he had become a sort of mascot, especially to the general medicine and neurology wards.

In spite of frequent spells in hospital for tests and high pressure, sometimes painful and exhausting physiotherapy—for there was always hope of a breakthrough—he was a cheerful, boisterous little boy, who charmed staff and patients alike. This included Sister Birdy, as the ward sister had been affectionately dubbed many years ago by a colleague.

'That lad,' she said frequently, 'is better than all the medicine in the world, but for pity's sake don't tell him— he's got a big enough opinion of himself as it is.'

But only in the nicest possible way, thought Holly.

'Young Billy's a gutsy kid, isn't he?' said a familiar voice from behind her.

Holly turned her head to find Ben's smiling face inches from her own. A little prickle of pleasure made the hairs on the back of her neck stand up as their eyes met. His were brim-full of laughter—dancing eyes.

Memories of last night flooded her mind for an instant. It had been a great evening, though not what she had expected after the build-up Jan had given him. But he's not called the registrar with the roving eye for nothing, she thought wryly, so watch it, my girl—don't go falling for him. You've been warned he's a dedicated bachelor and you'd only be another notch in his macho belt.

She brought herself back to earth and smiled up at him.

'He certainly is,' she replied, adding wistfully, 'Ben, will Billy ever walk again, do you think?'

The laughter in Ben's green-hazel eyes was replaced by a thoughtful expression. 'Well, the neuro bods seem to think there's an outside chance and they're not renowned for being over-optimistic. We'll have to wait and see what this latest batch of tests throws up and meanwhile press on with his physio. The important thing is never to give up hope. Billy's certainly got the right temperament to battle it out, with his parents' help and ours.'

He ran a hand through his thick mop of hair that was beginning to curl on his collar. 'I wish the same could be said for little Rennie Coles who came in to us yesterday— there's no fight left in her.'

'With abdominal pain and massive bruising, I dare say we wouldn't have any fight left in us if we'd been abused,' Holly said bitterly. 'Poor little girl, what must it be like to be six years old and never to have known any-thing but being beaten up?' She felt tears stinging the back of her eyes and turned her head away so that Ben wouldn't see them. It wasn't very professional.

Ben put an arm round her shoulders and squeezed hard. 'Difficult to be tough and detached, isn't it?' he said, his

voice warm and deep. 'I feel I could weep buckets sometimes at the things we see here. It's bad enough coping
with the natural accidents and diseases that attack the kids,
but the cases we get in which are the result of inflicted
injury…'

His hand squeezed even tighter on her shoulder. 'I have
nightmares about them sometimes.' There was a choked
note in his voice.

His hand still resting on her shoulder felt reassuring and
comforting. If they'd been anywhere else but in the ward
she would have turned round and given him a hug for
being so understanding. Who would have thought that the
teasing, fun-loving, laid-back Ben Harvey felt so deeply?
She knew him to be a good doctor, but imagined that he
easily 'switched off' when away from the hospital.

Though, come to think of it, she had glimpsed a little
of this side of him last night. But she had a strong feeling
that he didn't reveal this more serious side of his nature
very often, and felt privileged. 'Do you?' she murmured
softly. 'I'm glad.'

'Glad!' He dropped his hand and moved a step away.
His eyebrows arched questioningly halfway up his high,
broad forehead. 'You sound surprised. Why glad?'

'I…I…I'm not sure,' she stumbled out. She could
hardly say that she hadn't thought him capable of such
depths of feeling, it would be as good as saying that she
had thought him shallow.

'You've been listening to rumours,' he said dryly. 'You
think that what you see is all that you get. What's that
old saying about not judging a book by its cover?' His
mouth curled into a sardonic smile; his eyes were without
expression.

Holly felt her cheeks burning. 'I'm so sorry, I didn't mean to sound rude. You're a smashing doctor but...'

'You're not sure about the man?' Amusement flared in his eyes.

'I don't know him.'

'Not even after last night?' Now there was an expression that she couldn't fathom.

'We hardly had time to find out much about each other.'

'Then we'd better remedy that.' He touched her arm. 'Come out and have a drink with me tonight—there's a cosy little bar just round the corner.'

Her arm felt pleasantly warm where he touched it. 'I've heard about it. Their prices are through the roof—a couple of drinks and bang goes a month's salary.'

'So...it's my treat.'

'Well...'

'Please.' His eyes danced, but there was a hint of seriousness in their green depths.

She nodded. 'OK, I'm on till eight.'

'I'll pick you up in Reception at nine.'

'Fine.' She looked at her fob watch. 'Good Lord, I must get cracking on the medicines or I won't be finished before lunch-time.'

Ben pulled a face. 'And I, for my sins, must go and check up on Colin Weaver, and hope that he'll be co-operative today. Heaven preserve me from truculent teenagers.'

'Well, at least his mum's not in at the moment, so you may be able to get somewhere with him. For what it's worth, I think ne's a bit scared of her.'

'Yes, I get that impression, poor kid. If she's not there, maybe he'll open up a bit and we'll find out why he's constantly stuffing himself—I'm sure it's a case of comfort eating, but why? I'd better push off and do a bit of Sherlock Holmesing. I'm worried about young Colin—if we don't stabilise his weight, he's going to be in serious trouble.' And raising his hand in farewell, he strode off down the ward.

Holly watched his broad back disappear and felt a tingle of excitement. He had asked her out for a second time, though not to go dancing as he had promised last night, but at her instigation in order that they might to get to know each other better.

There was certainly more to Ben Harvey, the registrar with the roving eye, than rumour gave him credit for. There were depths in him to be plumbed, and she was determined that she was going to do the plumbing. He truly cared about his young patients, yet for some reason concealed it beneath a casual, throw-away front most of the time.

On and off during the rest of her busy day, as she persuaded reluctant children to take medicine, submit to injections and having dressings changed, his image kept intruding into her thoughts. That in itself was unusual, since through years of practice she had taught herself to put personal matters to one side when on duty. But for once the discipline failed to work and she kept finding herself on the verge of breaking into a smile. She couldn't wait for the evening to come.

'I feel bushed, but you look as fresh as a daisy,' said Jan Howard, when they met up at the nurses' station halfway through the afternoon. 'Could it be anything to do with our Ben and the after effects of last night?'

'Could be,' laughed Holly.

'You're seeing him again,' Jan accused. 'You watch it, my girl. He's a smashing guy, but he attracts girls like a magnet. If someone comes along with a better offer...'

CHAPTER TWO

IF SOMEONE comes along with a better offer! Jan's phrase repeated itself remorselessly in Holly's head as the hands on the wall clock above the reception counter moved past the half hour.

Conscious of the curious, or perhaps they were suspicious, eyes of the night receptionist and the security guard, neither of whom she knew, Holly moved away down the foyer and did another round of the shopping mall. At nine-thirty, the shops were all closed, but the windows were lit and there was a smattering of people around with whom she could mingle and be less conspicuous.

Holly eyed the people moving to and fro. They were mostly late visitors coming or going, but a few on-duty staff, recognisable by uniforms or badges, were using the bank of lifts in Reception to go about their business. But they were all strangers to her.

At a quarter to ten, having made allowances for the fact that Ben might have been held up on the wards, or called in to attend a patient in Accident and Emergency, she'd had enough. Well, he's not coming, she thought grimly. Clearly he's had a better offer. She felt foolish and embarrassed and her heart was a lead weight as she made her way back to the staff residence.

Common sense told her that only she knew that she had been stood up by Ben Harvey, but the feeling persisted that everyone was eyeing her with a sort of 'told you so' look.

24

Her thoughts alternated between hurt pride and anger. If he wanted to break their date, why the hell hadn't he told her straight out, or at the very least left a message for her? Just not to show up reeked of cowardice and bad manners, and after last night she wouldn't have thought him capable of either. As for the kind, caring doctor—surely he wouldn't behave that badly?

So, he wouldn't behave that badly, but he hadn't turned up, had he? If not another date, what had happened? In the act of unlocking her flat door, she stopped in her tracks…an accident! It was the one scenario she hadn't considered, she'd been so busy wallowing in self-pity. The possibility turned into a probability. He'd mentioned a flat somewhere the other side of the park, perhaps his taxi…or he might have walked—she had no idea of the distance.

Either way he could be lying somewhere badly injured. Hell! From what she had seen, London traffic was either at a standstill or taking incredible risks darting in front of each other, crossing lanes. In the dark, he could have been knocked down and… Her imagination leapt. She pictured pools of blood, head injuries, broken legs, unconsciousness, he might even be…

'No!' she said loudly. 'He can't be…not Ben, he's too, too alive.' Her heart was about to burst through her chest wall; she was breathing hard and painfully. For a moment she panicked, forgot she was a nurse. What should she do? Who should she tell? If he wasn't on duty, no one would know where he was. Only she knew that they were meeting—and Jan. But it could be hours before he was missed.

Her fingers shaking, Holly struggled with her key half in the lock. There were voices at the far end of the corridor, and she looked round to see Kent Summers, a house officer whom she'd met briefly and who seemed a nice guy, and Julie Coles, her next door neighbour, coming towards her.

Relief washed over her. She could talk to them, get their advice about whom to notify. They would know the drill.

She opened her mouth to speak, but Julie beat her to it. 'Have you seen the message for you on the telephone board?' she called.

'Message?' Holly repeated blankly.

'Yeah, someone took a call for you and stuck a notice on the board.'

Air rushed noisily out of Holly's lungs. 'Thanks,' she breathed, already a few steps down the corridor. 'I'll go and collect it.'

The note read, 'For Holly Brown—Call from BH—gorgeous voice—Sorry about tonight, something cropped up, be in touch, BH.'

Holly read it a dozen times. It never altered. Nothing to intimate what cropped up, how important it was, but at least he was sorry, or so he said, and would be in touch. Small comfort, but all she was going to get for the moment—but tomorrow... They would be on duty and at some point he would explain.

'And it had better be a damned good explanation,' she said into her pillow as she tried to get to sleep.

By ten o'clock the following morning he'd not appeared on the ward, though usually he made an early round before nine.

Holly was in the linen room collecting clean sheets and pillow cases when Sister Birdy popped her head round the door.

'Are you just going to bed bath little Rennie Coles, Holly?' she asked.

'Yes, Sister, I decided to do her myself and take one of the students with me. The poor little scrap is going to need very gentle handling—she's scared as well as being in pain. I suppose there's no more info about possible internal injuries?'

Sister shook her head. 'No, but maybe this second scan will reveal something. The one they did in A and E yesterday wasn't very clear. I want you to be with her when she goes for her scan. Meanwhile, it's good old-fashioned nursing. Accurate observations and constant reassurance and oodles of TLC. You're specialling her, Holly, it's down to you to win her confidence and try to find out what happened without further distressing her.'

'I heard that her mother was so badly beaten up she was unconscious when the ambulance crew got there.'

'Yes, she's been taken to The Royal George just down the road. Apparently a neighbour called the police because she heard screaming coming from the flat next door, and when they got there they called the ambulance. I understand that the police are waiting for the mother to recover consciousness, to question her.'

Sister Birdy compressed her lips and added in a tight voice, 'They wanted to speak to little Rennie, but I made it quite clear that she was too traumatised to be questioned, and Ben Harvey backed me up. Why, it doesn't even seem to have registered with the poor little mite that her mother's not around. We've got to be very patient and wait for her to make the first move.'

'Yes—Ben—Dr Harvey said that he didn't want to distress her by probing too much when he examined her yesterday, but perhaps he'll find out more when he sees her today.' Under cover of the pile of sheets she was holding, Holly crossed her fingers, perhaps Sister knew why he hadn't yet put in an appearance on the ward.

'I'm afraid we won't be seeing anything of our Dr Ben today, or for the foreseeable future, more's the pity. He's been called away on a personal matter—an accident, some sort of family crisis. We're going to miss him. Best registrar I've ever worked with and I've worked with a good many in my time.' She shook her head and ran fingers through her cropped, greying hair. 'Don't know who's going to cover for him yet, but he's a hard act to follow. Let's just hope that he won't be away too long.'

I second that, thought Holly fervently as she made her way to little Rennie's bed. Whatever could have happened that was to keep him away for an indefinite period? It must be something serious. Poor Ben, last night he hadn't had a care in the world, and today... She gave a contemptuous little snort. What the hell was she thinking of, worrying about Ben who was competent and resourceful and well able to take care of himself? Unlike little Rennie Coles.

Resolutely, she put Ben and the dozens of questions that Sister's news had thrown up firmly to the back of her mind. She would need all her skill and concentration to help the damaged little girl lying pale and terrified on the bed.

Rennie's eyes were closed and she was holding herself rigid when Holly reached her bedside.

'Rennie,' Holly said softly, stroking back a strand of hair from the waxen forehead and wincing at the cut lip and livid bruise on the small cheek. 'Nurse Jane and I are going to give you a wash and make you more comfortable.'

The little girl's eyelids flew open and she whimpered slightly. She seemed to shrink into the bed.

'Darling, we won't hurt you—see.' Holly reached up and adjusted the venous line trickling hydrating fluid and painkiller through the needle fixed in the back of the small hand. 'There's something in there to stop you hurting…promise. It helped you last night, remember?'

Rennie's dark brown eyes followed Holly's movements and some of the fear seemed to leave them.

'You won't touch my tummy, will you?' she whispered in a trembly voice, laying her free hand across her abdomen.

Holly shook her head. 'No, love,' she promised. 'Is that where you hurt most?'

Rennie's huge eyes filled with tears which spilled over and trickled down her cheeks. 'Yes…it hurt when…' her little throat worked as she tried to swallow her tears '…when he kicked me—and he kicked Mummy too.' Suddenly she sat bolt upright and stared wildly round the little curtained cubicle. She clutched Holly's arm. 'I want my mummy, where's my mummy?' Her voice rose to a wail.

Sister Birdy came hurrying from her office and two nurses sped over from the station. Holly put her arms round the shuddering little body and hugged her as well as she could without dislodging the drip and cannula.

She rocked her to and fro. 'Hush, poppet,' she murmured. 'Mummy's not very well at the moment and is in hospital being looked after just as we are looking after you. She'll come and see you as soon as she can.' She looked over the little girl's head at Sister Birdy and shook her own head slightly, pleading with her not to intervene.

Sister Birdy got the message, nodded and said softly, 'We'll leave you to it, Holly, take all the time you need. Call if you need me.' Beckoning to Jane and the two other nurses to go with her, she left the cubicle.

It took a while between hiccuping tears and constant reassurance before Holly coaxed most of the story out of the traumatised child. Her own stomach was tied up in knots by the time Rennie had finished relating how 'the man' had broken into the flat and attacked her and her mother. Kicking and punching them both and banging her mother's head on the floor.

'Do you know the man, Rennie?' Holly asked softly. She felt a little leap of excitement—if Rennie could name the man it would help the police trace him and put him behind bars where he belonged.

'No, but I think Mummy does.'

'What makes you think that, love?' asked Holly, feeling her skin crawl as all sorts of possibilities flashed through her mind.

''Cause she said that Martin sent him to…' she frowned '…to sort her out.'

'And who's Martin?'

'My daddy…least, he *was* my daddy, but he's not now.' Rennie buried her face against Holly's tunic, and said in a muffled voice, 'I'm glad he's not my daddy any more, I don't like him, but I love my mummy.' She sobbed, her tears warm against Holly's chest. 'When can I see my mummy?'

Holly was silent for a moment as she stroked the child's hair. Did this mean that the estranged husband was threatening his wife?

She took a deep breath. This was where someone more experienced than she would have to take over, like a specially trained police officer—or Ben with his special charisma. The thought flashed through her mind. Well, he wasn't here, but maybe now Rennie had begun to talk she could be persuaded to open up to someone else.

She dropped a kiss on top of the dark head and gently

laid her back against the pillow. 'As soon as I've finished washing you, poppet, I'm going to phone the hospital where Mummy is and find out how she's doing. She may not be able to come and see you yet, but perhaps she will be able to talk to you on the phone.'

By the time she went off duty, Holly was limp and ragged with exhaustion. It was emotional rather than physical exhaustion. It had been that sort of day. Starting with the disquieting news about Ben, about whom she had refused to think as she'd continued with the harrowing job of nursing Rennie.

With Sister Birdy's blessing, she had spent most of the day with her small patient, gaining her confidence, building on the rapport already established between them. Unlike some of the pundits—mostly senior admin staff with no medical or nursing experience, who advocated detachment and saw no reason for someone costing x pounds per hour to spend valuable time with a patient— Sister Birdy believed in her nurses becoming involved with their patients.

'We are *not*,' she said frequently, often when going through the report at hand-over, 'in spite of the paperwork we have to do, clerks in an office adding up figures. Nor are we technicians, though we have to fiddle with a lot of gadgets. We're nurses dedicated to caring for our patients. And *that*, please remember, means hands-on nursing, and I don't want anyone on my staff who is not prepared to do that.'

As far as Holly could see, everyone in General Medicine did just that, and she was over the moon to be working with such a caring bunch of people. These sentiments matched her own. But today had certainly stretched her, and it was with relief that she let herself into her flat.

She was dying for a cup of tea—actually, she amended, she was dying for a glass of wine or a G and T, but, since she hadn't had time to stock up on anything in the drinks line, tea would have to do. She took herself off to the kitchen at the end of the corridor—mercifully empty, she had no wish to socialise. She made herself a large pot and took it back to her flat.

Thinking of wine brought Ben and their dinner at The Greenhouse sharply into focus. What a lovely evening that had been. It had promised so much. They had jelled together from the word go. Remembering how they had talked and laughed and flirted mildy, she felt her heart do a curious little flip. Knowing he was not in the hospital, she felt suddenly bereft. Where was he? What was he doing? What sort of family crisis had he been called away to deal with?

As far as she knew from the potted history he had divulged the other night, he didn't have much in the way of family. Apart from a few scattered octogenarian great-aunts and great-uncles, there were just his twin brother, Josh, his sister-in-law, Anthea, and his niece and nephew, Beth and James. They were all who really mattered to him.

Holly went cold suddenly. Supposing something had happened to one of them? Ben would be shattered. He had spoken of them almost fiercely with great warmth and affection.

'My brother and I are totally unalike in everything,' he'd said. 'He's a businessman through and through, has shares in an airline and a finger in a dozen financial pies, whereas I'm a complete dunderhead where business is concerned. But he's my best friend as well as being my twin—and I'm godfather to Beth and James. They're all the family I need.' Then he added to her surprise, 'I'd like you to meet them one day, Holly.'

'I'd love that,' she'd replied, a warm glow spreading through her at the idea that he wanted her to meet them.

It's sad, she'd thought, that he has such a small family when I'm up to my ears in brothers and sisters. OK, so they can be a pain sometimes, she'd added to herself wryly, but, my God, I wouldn't be without them for anything. When the chips are down, they're there for me, whereas Ben…

Impulsively, she had reached across the table and touched his fingers clasped round his wineglass. 'I know you're not looking for commitment at present,' she'd said, 'and I can understand that, but at some time in the future wouldn't you like to marry and have kids of your own? You're so brilliant with the smallies on the ward.'

He'd looked at her very hard for a moment and she'd wondered if she'd blown the entire evening, since it had been an off-limits remark to make. He'd made it quite clear at the outset how he felt about commitment.

Then quite suddenly he'd laughed a deep throaty laugh, and his eyes had twinkled. 'Why?' he'd countered. 'Are you offering yourself as a candidate for this far-off nuptial, blissful future with the world's most famous paediatric consultant? I warn you, I'll be the most demanding, chauvinistic husband and lover.'

Holly had rolled her eyes dramatically. 'Heaven forbid,' she'd chuckled. 'The last person on earth I'd marry would be a dedicated doctor, consultant or not. Anyway, I'm a dedicated career woman. *If* I marry, it will be strictly on a fifty-fifty basis, everything from the kitchen sink to…'

'Changing nappies,' he'd replied with a lovely lopsided

grin. 'Thanks, but no, thanks, I'll stick with Josh's family and fatherhood once removed.'

They had laughed together then, and the rest of the evening had been as light and frothy and inconsequential as it had started out.

Or had it? Holly stared down into her mug of tea. Hadn't there been a sort of undercurrent of things not said? She gave herself a brisk mental shake. No! No! No! She was letting her imagination run riot—the evening had ended as it had begun, casually, and with a goodnight kiss brushed across her cheek.

So why did she feel bereft because he wasn't around? Don't know, she answered herself brusquely. But at least he had said that he would be in touch—that was some comfort.

If he gets in touch, a demon voice whispered.

CHAPTER THREE

IT WAS more than three weeks before Ben got in touch.

Holly had just come off duty one night when someone banged on her door. 'Call for you,' a voice shouted. 'Man with a sexy voice, like honey.'

Instinct and the description, told her it was Ben. He certainly had a sexy voice. The hairs on the back of her neck stood up on end; her mouth went dry. He'd kept his promise when she'd almost given him up. She raced along the hall to the phone.

'Ben,' she said breathlessly when she picked up the receiver.

There was a moment's silence—then he said, gruffly, 'Holly... How did you know it was me?'

His voice didn't sound right: sexy it might be, but it also sounded strained, tired. Not surprising considering what he'd been through.

Her own voice was hesitant. How much would he expect her to know? 'I don't know, I just sort of guessed— and you said you'd be in touch...' Her own voice cracked. 'But, oh, Ben, I've been so worried about you... How are you?'

There was another silence, then, 'I take it the grapevine's been busy.'

'Yes.'

'What does it say?'

Holly took in a deep breath—supposing the grapevine had got it wrong? Not that it had, Sister Birdy had confirmed most of the rumours. 'That your brother and his wife were…' She couldn't finish the sentence.

'Killed in an accident?' It sounded as if he was speaking through clenched teeth.

'Yes… Oh, Ben, I'm so very sorry—for you and for the children. I haven't been able to get you out of my mind. If there's anything—*anything*—I can do, you only have to say.'

He gave a stark bark of laughter. 'You can meet me for a drink one evening, the sooner the better. I won't be much company, but I owe you a drink, don't I? You might say that I stood you up for our last date.'

Now he sounded hard, brittle, most un-Ben like. Holly heard the agony in his voice.

It was a piercing cry for help. 'Tomorrow night,' she said. 'Seven o'clock. Just tell me where.' She knew he wouldn't want to come to Lizzie's. She hoped he wouldn't choose The Greenhouse, that was too special.

'The Lamb, Fountain Square. It's a decent pub, my local. I'll send a taxi for seven.'

'There's no need, I can—'

'I'll send a cab.' His voice was like steel.

'But…'

'Tomorrow, seven, The Lamb.' His phone clicked off.

Sometimes the day dragged—sometimes it galloped. Much of the time, Holly went round like a robot, her mind whirring, you're seeing Ben tonight—you're seeing Ben tonight like a stuck disc. Through habit and practice she was able to damp down the insistent voice and go about her tasks with her usual efficiency, and an abundance of warmth and tenderness.

Methodically she worked her way through the list of patients she was specialling and at eleven o'clock had reached Alice Fisher's bed. Alice was in what had been little Rennie Coles's bed until a few days before, when she had been re-united with her mother.

Ironically, Alice too was suffering from abdominal pain, though not inflicted, as in Rennie's case, by a man's boot.

Holly glanced at the girl's admission notes. The ten-year-old girl had been admitted late the day before with abdominal pain, query appendicitis. Alternatively, the doctor who had examined her on admission, had scribbled: 'This well-developed just-ten-year-old might be having problems with precocious puberty, and the onset of her menstrual cycle. Neither mother, who accompanied her, nor child, very communicative.'

He'd ordered ultra-sound imaging of ovaries and uterus, as well as a general abdominal scan and obs to eliminate or confirm either diagnosis—or perhaps something even more obscure. Meanwhile, as a precaution, he had instructed nil by mouth, fluids by IV line *in situ*.

Holly checked that the drip was running at the prescribed rate, and smiled down at the girl.

'How are you feeling today, Alice?' she asked gently.

Alice didn't smile, but stared contemptuously back at Holly.

''Ow the 'ell do you think I feel?' she muttered.

'Lousy, I should think,' replied Holly.

Surprised, the girl blinked and focused on Holly's name and rank badge, pinned to her white tunic top.

'Why are you called 'olly?' Curious—not so truculent.

'Because I was born on Christmas Eve and my mum had been out gathering the holly for decorating the house.'

'What d'ya mean, *gathering* the 'olly?' Alice frowned, there was a little colour in her cheeks and she sounded...intrigued.

Holly was pleased. Thank God she'd got some sort of response. 'From the hedges round the fields. I live on a farm, holly and mistletoe grow wild in the hedges.'

'Blooman 'ell, our mum gets ours from Tesco's.'

'Well, somebody has to grow it,' said Holly. 'Now keep quiet for five minutes while I take your temperature, pulse and blood pressure.'

Apart from wincing occasionally and drawing her legs up slightly, Alice lay quiet as the routine observations were taken, but her eyes didn't leave Holly's face.

'Well, what does all that tell ya?' she wanted to know when Holly had finished.

'That your temperature and blood pressure are within normal limits, though your pulse is a little fast, but nothing to worry about.'

'So I'm OK, then, I can go 'ome?'

Holly shook her head, 'Sorry, love, not yet. We've still got to find out what's causing this pain. It was pretty bad when you came in last night.'

'Yeah, well, it ain't so bad now and I want to be at 'ome with me mum and the others.' The belligerence was back. 'And I wanta know why I can't 'ave anything t'eat or drink.'

'Because until you have some tests we don't know what's causing this pain. You've been sick several times, which may mean that there could be something wrong anywhere between here and here.' Holly ran her index finger down the girl's throat to her lower abdomen. 'It's the tube down which you swallow and digest your food— it's called the alimentary tract.'

'But I 'urts mostly down 'ere.' Alice stroked her hand across the very lowest part of her abdomen just above the pubic area. 'And it sorta comes in waves, like, and when it's very bad, well, that's when I'm sick—that's what I told the doc last night, but 'e didn't seem to get me meaning, just talked about scans and things.'

It flitted through Holly's mind that, had Ben examined this child, although there was a limit to what a ten-year-old could understand, he would have found a way of explaining to Alice what might be wrong. Certainly from her own description, it looked more and more like the early onset of puberty.

Yet obviously the doctor, whoever he was—the scribbled signature on the report, looking like the demented scratching of a cat, didn't give anything away—hadn't seen fit to inform Alice of the possibility of her menstrual cycle starting. Perhaps there was a good reason for that.

So I can hardly suggest it, thought Holly, resolving as she made a note of Alice's description in the report to have a word with Sister Birdy when she'd finished her round.

To Alice she said gently, 'That's why you're having several different tests, love, in case it's something else and nothing to do with your food tract or your appendix.'

'So when am I gonna 'ave these tests?'

'This afternoon. They don't take long and they don't hurt,' Holly reassured. 'Now, love, can I get you more magazines or a puzzle or anything before I go?'

Alice ignored that. 'Will you be coming with me this afternoon?' She looked suddenly pathetic and very young, the bravado gone. 'Me mum can't get 'ere till this evening.'

Holly squeezed her hand. 'I'll be there,' she said, crossing her fingers that she would be able to square it with Sister Birdy.

Out of the blue, Billy Bowman came whizzing up and parked himself by Alice's bed.

'Hi, kid, what you in for?' he asked Alice. He looked

at the notice above her bed, and read out, 'Nil by mouth.'
He shook his carroty, bristly head mournfully. 'That
means you can't have anything to eat or drink. That's like
when you have an operation—it's the worst part. I've had
a lot of operations—ops, the nurses call them.' He grinned
up at Holly, and then at Alice. 'Have you had an op?'

'No, and what's with this kid business?' Alice murmured, staring at him with suspicious eyes in which there
was a reluctant flicker of interest. 'I'm years older than
you, and, anyway, I bet you ain't 'ad loads of operations—what were they all for, then?'

Billy looked pleased with himself; he'd got an audience. 'To take out a lump in my head, a tumour it's called,
just here,' he said, doing a wheelie on his rear wheels and
indicating the back of his head. 'There's a scar but my
hair's practically covered it now.'

'So 'ow come you 'ad something done to your 'ead and
you can't walk?'

'The lump was pressing on…'

Grinning to herself, Holly slipped out of the cubicle
and moved on to her next patient with the curious feeling
that she had left Alice in good hands. As Sister Birdy
said, Billy was better than any medicine.

Are you all right, Holly?' Jan asked when they were halfway through the medicine round a little later. 'If you don't
mind my saying, you look a bit the worse for wear—bad
night?'

Holly pulled a face. 'You could say that,' she said
wryly.

Jan looked at her with shrewd, intelligent eyes. 'It's our
Ben Harvey, isn't it? Even though he's not here you can't
get him out of your mind, can you?' There was a look of
concern on Jan's kind, motherly face. 'Look, love, you

had one date with him and might have had another if this terrible tragedy hadn't overtaken him. And at this moment, of course, you feel especially sorry for him—we all do—and he said he'd get in touch, but don't expect too much. After all, it's been several weeks since the accident.'

'He's been in touch, he phoned last night, and I'm meeting him tonight. Oh, Jan.' Holly paused as she carefully measured out a dose of medicine. 'He sounded terrible—desperately sad, of course, but somehow defeated, bitter, unsure of himself.'

'Well, he's got an awful lot on his plate, love, you know, he's probably handling his brother's affairs. From what he's said from time to time, I know he and his brother were close, and he was crackers about his brother's kids, pleased as Punch that he was their godfather. I remember when little James was born, he used to bore us to death about his progress through first tooth to first word.'

She frowned as she poured water into a tumbler and stirred in some powder. 'I wonder who'll be responsible for those two now that they've lost their parents?' She gave the orange liquid a final stir. 'Now to go and do battle with our difficult teenager,' she said. 'You'd think that I was giving him poison instead of something to stop his bowels blocking up again. You'd almost think he wanted another enema.'

'It's all that rubbish his silly mum and dad smuggle in to him,' Holly murmured absently as Jan crossed to Colin's bed. 'They think we're starving him.' She ticked Colin Weaver off on the chart, and thought bleakly, They may be silly but at least he has parents who love him, whereas Beth and James… Who will take care of them now that their parents are dead?

*   *   *

'I will. I've been appointed Beth and James's guardian,' Ben told her a few hours later in answer to Holly's tentative question. 'So it's all down to me, and I love them to bits, but I don't know how the hell I'm going to cope— make up to them for…' he cleared his throat '…them losing Josh and Anthea. They were wonderful parents. To tell you the truth, I'm not coping very well with what's happened on my own account—Josh and I… Kirsty's been wonderful, but…'

Kirsty, Holly recalled, was the young 'au pair stroke nanny' he'd mentioned on that evening at The Greenhouse.

'But the three of them stand and look at me sometimes with their big eyes, willing me to work a miracle and bring Josh and Anthea back. It totally shatters me. I think Beth understands that her parents are dead, but James, he keeps asking me when they are coming back.' He balled his fists till the knuckles showed white.

He and Holly were sitting side by side on a high-backed oak settle in The Lamb. He looked incredibly worn and haggard; there were lines about his mouth and eyes that hadn't been there before. And the habitual twinkle had gone out of his eyes—they were a dull green, shadowed by sadness. But it wasn't just the physical changes that were apparent; the whole man had changed.

Gone was the fun-loving, caring medic looking younger than his years but brimming over with confidence and assurance. In his place an uptight, unsure man looking years older, faced with a problem he didn't seem to have the strength to deal with.

Holly put a small hand over his larger one and stroked the white knuckles.

'You'll cope.' She made her voice confident. 'Don't try to replace Josh and Anthea with the kids, just be yourself, their loving uncle, the man they're used to. And don't be afraid to talk about their parents to them, and let them talk to you. They may get distressed, but it is less dangerous than keeping it bottled up.'

She stopped massaging his hand and, picking up her glass, took a sip of wine. Very matter-of-factly, she said, 'Ben, you will have to explain over and over again to James that Mummy and Daddy have died but they are now safe in heaven. The concept might be difficult for you to grasp, but it is something that James will understand, find comforting.'

'That's what Mrs Kelly says. She talks about going to the angels and all that sort of thing.'

'Who's Mrs Kelly.'

'Our daily cook-housekeeper, she came to Josh and Anthea when they were first married. She's sixtyish and cuddly and very fond of the kids.'

A housekeeper and a nanny, so at least there was no shortage of cash in this otherwise bereft household.

'And a wise old thing by the sound of it,' said Holly. 'She knows that until James accepts that his parents aren't coming back, he'll always be waiting for them to come through the door. He has to know that that won't happen, but he also has to know that they are happy wherever they are.' And so do you, she thought, looking at his gaunt face, pale beneath a light tan.

She knew that she was telling him this for his sake as much as the children's. She must get him to go on talking, release the pressure inside him. He'd made a start, but he needed to talk more and he was a man in need of all the help that she could give him.

His appearance had shocked her when they'd met half an hour before. He looked years older than thirty-something—nearer to forty. The smooth golden tan had all but disappeared, and he was definitely thinner. Not surprising, she realised, when she heard how the news of his brother and sister-in-law's deaths had been broken to him—by the local police. His brother's plane had crashed in France, there had been a pilot and one passenger, believed to be Joshua and Anthea Harvey.

'I was asked to go over and identify the bodies,' Ben said, his face whitening further at the memory. 'Well, you must have seen enough accident victims. They were terribly smashed up, hard to recognise, their faces...' A shudder went through him and beer splashed on the table.

Holly squeezed his free hand. *This* is what he wants, *needs* to talk about, instinct prompted her.

'Their injuries must have been horrendous,' she said, keeping her voice calm. 'How did the accident happen? Did it resemble an RTA?' Let it all out, she begged silently, give it to me in graphic detail.

Ben took a great gulp of beer, staring at her over the rim of the glass. 'Worse,' he ground out, 'because of the height. They lost control and spiralled down—hit the ground nose on...you can imagine, the worst of impact injuries—faces squashed, pulped to nothingness almost, hair streaked with blood and their necks broken.'

With exaggerated care he placed his glass on the table and turned towards Holly. He took hold of her hands, rubbing his thumbs across her knuckles. 'I dream about it every night, can't get it out of my head. I haven't told anybody, couldn't, not even old friends, but you...it's easy to talk to you, Holly.'

His dark, shadowed, pain-filled eyes swept over her face and came to rest on her mouth. He leaned forward and kissed her, his lips firm and cold, too cold—marble-like—pressed against hers. 'Can we do this again, just meet and talk?'

Heart bumping unevenly, Holly kissed him firmly back. She was proud that he felt he could unload to her, when he had other older friends in whom he might have confided, but she was also a touch scared. Was she taking on more than she could manage, acting as counsellor as well as friend? She knew so little about him. She had felt so confident a few minutes before, but now…would she do more harm than good? Shouldn't he be talking to a trained counsellor?

Her mum would say, 'What are friends for but to offer a shoulder to cry on when in need?'

She looked into Ben's eyes, felt his cold hands holding onto hers as if he were drowning. Here was a friend in need, all right. She leaned forward and kissed him on the mouth again.

'Of course,' she said softly. 'We can meet any time you want whenever I'm free. I'm all yours, Ben.'

For an instant there was a flicker of amusement in his eyes. 'I should be so lucky,' he said.

Half an hour later he put her into a cab. Before closing the door, he cupped her face in his hands and kissed her again.

'Thanks for everything,' he murmured against her cheek. 'And I'll think over what you said about getting back to work soon. You could be right, maybe I've been smothering the kids, and re-establishing some sort of routine will be the best thing for them.' He rubbed the tip of his nose to hers. It seemed more intimate than the kiss, she thought. He smiled—it was a poor thing compared to his usual smile, but a smile none the less. 'You are wise beyond your years, my child.'

For the first time that evening, reminded of Alice and her exchange with Billy, Holly allowed herself to chuckle.

'Who are you calling a child?' she said. 'You're no Methusclah yourself.' In fact, he was looking fractionally better than when she had arrived. He was less drawn, less haggard—offering her shoulder had been the right thing to do.

Ben smiled another shaky smile. 'All due to my own good Samaritan,' he murmured.

'And like the Samaritans, we're on call at all hours—except when on duty. You've got my mobile number, use it whenever… Goodnight, Ben. Go home and sleep well; no nightmares tonight.'

She watched him out of the rear window, standing in the light streaming out from the pub as the cab drew away. He looked very solitary and for two pins she would have stopped the taxi and hurried back to give him a hug. But she didn't.

She didn't, because, in spite of the way he had confided in her, she wasn't quite sure how he felt about her, or, for that matter, how she felt about him. The man she had dated, what seemed aeons ago, was a different creature from the man she had met tonight. This man needed her and brought out all her nursing and maternal instincts, but he was almost a stranger. And she was flattered, touched to be chosen as his confidant but…

Anyway, there would be plenty of time for hugs and kisses at some time in the future. That there would be a future, in spite of Jan's warnings and her own reservations, she was quite sure, but how it would end, she was less sure.

Certainly the man she had talked to tonight was not the same man as the one who had wined and dined her at The Greenhouse. He was not the legendary registrar with the roving eye; he was a profoundly shocked man with immense responsibilities, struggling to come to terms with soul-deep grief. But, just as she'd been attracted to the fun-loving young medic, this other side of the man attracted her too. Humbly she prayed that, with her help, he would make it.

'So, how did last night go?' Jan asked when at last she caught up with Holly in the toddlers' bay, where they were supervising the year-plus infants eating their dinners. They were enveloped in plastic aprons, and half their time was spent avoiding globs of mashed-up vegetables zooming past their ears as small, wobbly hands seemed hell bent on using their carefully cooked food as ammunition.

Holly bent over the tiny fifteen-month-old infant she was helping to feed. Tiny because she had an absorption problem with her food following a liver bypass operation. The operation had been successful and would hold off a liver transplant until she was older, or, if she was enormously lucky, perhaps even permanently.

Until a week ago, little Dawn Platt had had a long spell on the liver ward with other critically ill babies receiving specialist treatment. Now she was thought fit enough to be nursed on General Medicine, where the less tense atmosphere would help her towards full convalescence, though she was still on a strict regime of a cocktail of sophisticated drugs and a carefully planned, nourishing diet.

'Come on, Dawn, love, just one more mouthful and then we'll have our pudding,' Holly pleaded.

Dawn shook her head, clamped her lips together and, grabbing the spoon from Holly's hand, sent it and its high protein/carbohydrate contents sailing down to the other end of the table.

Jan, who was crouching between two small boys who were waging battle with each other, ducked too late and caught spoon and contents smack in the face. The ring of toddlers in their high chairs chortled. Dawn clapped her hands and giggled. Jan wiped away most of the mixture with a tissue and waved the spoon at her.

'You little horror,' she sang out. 'You're certainly on the mend.'

'Isn't she just?' laughed Holly, giving the fragile child a hug and planting a kiss on top of her head. 'Good shot, poppet.' A few days ago, she thought, she wouldn't have had the strength or the inclination to flip anything that far—just shows what a bit of TLC and patience can do. 'Now, what about some pudding? Banana and custard— doesn't that smell good?' She held the dish under the little nose.

Dawn looked at her and then at the spoon with big saucer eyes and then opened her mouth wide. Holly popped in a spoonful as she thought carefully about what to say to Jan about her meeting with Ben. No way did she want to portray too dismal an image, Ben would hate that, but she did want to convey the fact that he was not the playboy that he had been.

Between wiping mouths and small hands, Jan repeated her unanswered question. 'So, how did it go last night?'

'Well, as you suspected, Ben has been frantically busy sorting out his brother's affairs. Apparently they're very complex—his brother was a high-flyer and pretty rich.'

'Yes, so I believe. Ben used to say that his brother had all the business brains in the family, though I think he exaggerated a bit. Our Ben's not short on brains himself, he just chose medicine instead of business, thank God. We need medics like him.' Jan raised her eyes heaven- wards and tut tutted as she removed a dollop of pudding from a small ear.

'*This*, poppet, is your mouth,' she said, guiding a

chubby hand in the right direction before resuming her questioning. 'But how was Ben in himself? He must be feeling gross, shattered—losing a twin must be like losing half of one's self. I should think even his ability to bounce back is pretty stretched. It's the sort of thing that could change him for life.'

Holly said softly, 'He should have talked to you, Jan, rather than me. You know him so well.'

'Inevitable—we've worked together for nearly five years, and you know how it is, you get pretty close—especially on nights, propping each other up...' she gave a rather grim little smile '...physically and emotionally, watching over a kid who is at death's door, you either get to be real buddies, or...'

'Yeah, I know how it is... Jan, you don't mind, do you, that Ben wanted to see me, rather than you?'

'*Mind!* Of course not. You're a free agent and I'm not, for one thing, and I'm far too ancient for another. I'd say that Ben needs a smidgen of mothering and a hell of a lot of loving of the sort I can't give him right now, and, for all that you've only just met, you seem to fit the bill. So get cracking, woman, and do your stuff.'

'The sort of loving I can't give him,' Holly mused out loud, recalling the conversation she'd had with Jan. 'For that, read sex.'

Is that what Ben wants, needs right now? She massaged shampoo savagely into her scalp, then tipped her head this way and that under the shower to rinse it off. I think he's more into the mothering bit, and I'm not sure that I want to...perhaps later—much later...

She exhaled her breath in a long sigh—funny, he had dated her originally, and she had accepted it, because they had both been footloose and fancy-free and wanted to remain so. Yet here she was, going in at the deep end, committing herself to being friend and confidante. Even if she wanted an out, she wasn't sure that there was one. Though, come to that, she wasn't sure that she would take it if there were. So much for footloose and fancy-free.

Her mobile buzzed insistently. She turbaned her hair and wrapped herself in a large towel. It's probably Mum, she thought, wanting a blow-by-blow account of my social life over the last few days. I might tell her about meeting Ben last night. I'd value her input. She smiled as she picked up the mobile. Clever old thing, Mum, doesn't push but…

It wasn't her mum—it was Ben.

'You were right, Holly,' he said the minute she switched on. 'About getting things back to normal. I took Beth and James to school this morning and they were almost like their old selves. Came home full of what they'd been doing.' There was a pause. 'James drew a picture of a plane—said it was Josh's.' He faltered. 'I told him what had happened, that Josh's plane had crashed…'

'And?'

'He didn't say anything, just looked at me. So I explained again that they'd been badly hurt in the crash, too hurt for the doctors to help them, but that they were happy and safe in heaven. And after a moment he asked, "Are they with the angels?" And I simply said yes. Bloody hell, Holly, how can you explain death to a four-year-old?'

'In the way that you did, Ben. Sounds as if you made a good job of it. And what about Beth? Was she there when this was going on?'

'Oh, yes. She was a bit tearful, but she said very firmly that of course Mummy and Daddy were with the angels and they were happy. You and Mrs Kelly were right, that worked. We had a sort of nursery tea all together in the kitchen and talked about Josh and Anthea, and actually laughed a bit. The kids amazed me by remembering all sorts of things that had happened in the past, funny little things that had stuck in their memories...'

There was a pause, and then he added, 'And it's all down to you, Holly, giving me a push in the right direction. I was knee-deep in self-pity. Getting back to school has worked wonders for the kids and I'm going to get off my backside and get back to work—stat. You can expect me bright and early tomorrow, for, as we're all fond of saying, life must go on.'

Holly's heart gave a little bump—was there a hint of sarcasm in his voice? 'Oh, Ben, that is good news. It'll be lovely to have you back—we need you: the kids, all of us. Jan was saying today how much you're missed.'

Ben drew in a long, deep breath. 'Well, I just hope that I'm up to the job and don't let down either you or Jan, or of course the kids.'

'You won't,' Holly reassured firmly. 'Once you get stuck in, you'll be your old self.'

CHAPTER FOUR

BOB ROPER was taking the report from the night staff nurse, Clair Thompson, when Holly arrived on duty the following morning.

He nodded across at a curtained cubicle opposite the nurses' station. 'Guess who's over there,' he murmured.

Holly's heart did a little flip. She could have made a good guess but decided against it. Only Jan knew that Ben had been in touch with her, and even she didn't know that Ben had decided to return to work so soon. 'I'm right out of guesses. Tell me.' she said.

'Our Ben,' replied Bob triumphantly. 'He was here when I arrived a few minutes ago. Looks a bit ragged, not his usual bouncy self, which isn't surprising, poor chap. But it's still good to see him; the place isn't the same without him.'

I second that, thought Holly fervently. She pinned a surprised expression on her face. 'Oh, that is good news. Sister Birdy didn't seem to think he would be back for a while yet. Of course, I only worked with him for a few days before he went on compassionate leave, but it was enough to see that he was brilliant with the kids.'

'And hasn't lost his touch,' Clair said. 'He arrived just as a new little admission was shuttled up from A and E, query streptococcal pneumonia. She should have gone to Chests, but they're crammed full. Poor kid, she was scared and breathless as one might expect, but Ben stepped in and began to work his usual magic and calmed her down.

He's examining her now. The parents are in the family room, he said he'd speak to them when he'd finished.'

Holly decided to be bold. She looked at Bob who was standing in till Sister Birdy arrived. 'Shall I go and see if he wants a hand? I can read the report later.'

'Good idea, and you could carry on specialling her for the rest of the day.' He glanced down at the admission card. 'Her name's Jessica Dench, aged seven.'

Ben was sitting on the side of the bed holding Jessica's hand and talking quietly to her. His reddish chestnut-brown head was bent over her at an almost protective angle, as if willing her to be reassured. It was a familiar poise when he was talking or listening to the children— intimate, friendly yet casual.

This was how she had seen him bending over other small patients in the few days they had worked together. It's as if he's never been away, Holly thought. But the thought died when he became aware of her presence and turned his head to look at her.

His eyes gave him away. There was a wary, cautious look in them that hadn't been there in the cheerful young medic of a few weeks ago—though she fancied that they weren't quite as bleak and defeated as they had been when she had first met him in the pub the other night.

Maybe that was due to her urging him back to work as he had claimed when he'd phoned last night. Not that the awful hurt and loss he had suffered were going to be healed by a well meant bit of advice—they went far too deep for that. At best it was a Band-Aid job. But perhaps it was the beginning of his coming to terms with his trauma and fighting back.

The terrible defeatism that she had witnessed that first night she had met him in the pub appeared to have vanished. So perhaps her little homily had done some good, and, surely, persuading him back to work had to be a plus.

But though this Ben, sitting holding a little girl's hand, might still be able to work his doctor magic on the kids, he wouldn't be able to conceal his pain from his colleagues. It would be only too apparent to those who knew him. The change was too marked. As Bob had said, his bounce—that was his trade mark—had gone. For all that he was hell-bent on reassuring the little girl on the bed, he looked as if he could do with a bit of reassurance himself.

Holly's heart went out to him, and the feeling that she'd had the other night that he was in need of a good solid hug more than anything made her catch her breath. Her galloping thoughts must have been reflected in her face, for Ben produced a crooked smile and gave her the thumbs-up sign as if to confirm that all was well.

'Hi there,' he said.

'Hi. It's good to see you.'

'Good to be back.' He transferred his smile to the child. 'I'm just explaining to Jess that her chest and shoulder hurts and she's feeling hot and uncomfortable because her lungs are full of gungy stuff that shouldn't be there.'

'Why is there gungy stuff in my lungs?' whispered Jess breathily, between the rapid, grunting respirations typical of her type of pneumonia.

It was the sort of go-straight-to-the-point question that children asked. Nothing daunted, Ben, acting on his principle that children were capable of discussing their own condition, and where possible frankness was the best policy, explained further. 'Because you have an infection called streptococcal pneumonia, which produces fluid in the tiny spaces in the lungs which should contain air. Quite a thought, isn't it?'

The small chest rose and fell rapidly; the breathy voice quavered. 'Can you make it go away and the air get back in?' The huge eyes in the flushed face pleaded.

Ben nodded and squeezed her hand. 'Certainly can, love, and quite quickly. You will be having some medicine called penicillin, which kills off the bugs fast.' He stood up. 'Now I'm going to leave you with Nurse Holly, here. She'll take good care of you.' He flicked another uneven smile at Holly.

He seems to specialise in crooked smiles, she thought. They're a remnant of the old Ben—minus the laughing eyes. But even without the laughing eyes, the crooked smile had a curious effect on her that she knew she must try to ignore. Now was definitely not the time to analyse her responses to this changed man. She had work to do.

She moved over to the bed and said softly, 'Hello, Jess, I'll be looking after you today.' She laid a hand on the child's forehead. 'My word, you are hot and sweaty. Now that Doctor's finished with his examination, I'm going to sponge you down and put you into clean night clothes. That'll make you feel fresher. And the medicine that Dr Ben's going to give you starts working from the first dose, so you'll soon be feeling heaps better. How does that sound?'

'Brill,' Jess murmured through her painful respirations, even managing a quavery smile. Then quite suddenly, reverting to the small girl that she was, her mouth trembled and she shrilled out in a panicky voice, 'When can I see my mummy? I want my mummy and daddy.'

Ben said cheerfully, 'You can see them in a few minutes, love, when Nurse Holly has given you the once-over. I'm going to have a chat with them right now and put them in the picture.' He stood up and moved to the foot of the bed. 'Trust the nurses and trust me kiddo,

you're going to be OK.' Then, with a wink and a wave
of his hand, he disappeared round the curtains.

He was back in the next instant.

'Hell, I need my brains tested,' he muttered to Holly.
'Nearly committed the unforgivable sin of not charting
Jess's medication.' He unhooked the clipboard from the
foot of the bed. 'I want her on half-hourly obs pro tem,
and paracetamol syrup as well as penicillin—that and the
tepid sponging should bring her temp down in a few
hours.' He scribbled on the chart as he spoke.

Then, pulling a sad clown's face to amuse Jess but
which spoke volumes to Holly, he said lightly, 'Sorry
about that, ladies, won't disturb you again.' And, with a
salute, disappeared and didn't return.

Holly didn't see anything of him for the next hour or so—
their paths didn't cross. He was busy covering the surgical
beds across the wide corridor, whilst she was working on
the medical side.

'For our sins,' Sister Birdy had explained to her on her
first day, 'General Medicine covers both surgical and
medical cases that don't qualify for specialist care in one
of the other departments. I rotate my nurses on a weekly
basis, so that they are familiar with the patients on both
sides. Like yourself, the senior staff are experienced in
both surgical and medical paediatric nursing.'

She had wrinkled her prominent bony nose. 'We also
take in various waifs and strays, kids waiting to go to or
coming from other departments.' Her mouth had twitched
at one corner. 'That's why we're sometimes called the
bric-à-brac ward—we're full of odds and ends.' Her grin
had broadened. 'But that's what makes life interesting if
you can stand the pace. So what do you think, Holly?
Will you be able to stand the pace?' She had tilted her

head at an enquiring angle, looking very like the bird she'd been named for.

'Sure can, Sister, try me.' Holly had beamed the older woman one of her happy smiles. 'I don't want to sound over-confident, but a ward full of odds and ends holds no fears for me. I can't wait to get stuck in.'

Sister had inspected her with sharp eyes, then nodded decisively. 'Yes, I think you'll do,' she'd said. 'Just remember, it's kids first, last and all the time when you're on duty. If you've got any personal problems, squash 'em or bring them to me and we'll thrash them out. Don't let them interfere with your work. Dedication and concentration are the name of the game when you're on my ward.'

Now over a month into her probationary period, Holly knew that she had so far lived up to Sister Birdy's expectations. Even over the last few weeks when she had been concerned for Ben, she had worked with her usual enthusiasm, had never let her personal feelings get the better of her. But this morning…

She let out a faint sigh. She couldn't get Ben's sad clown's face out of her mind, play-acting as he had been for Jess's benefit. It had been a cover-up for his frustration with himself for forgetting to chart Jessica's medication. A broken hearted clown, she thought, recalling vividly the painful expression in his eyes that had dimmed the twinkling hazel green.

He had managed to conceal it from Jess, and would, she guessed, manage to keep it hidden from the other children. A wry thought struck her: he would succeed in keeping his sadness hidden from all the kids, with the exception of Billy Bowman.

Bright, intelligent, perceptive boy that he was, he would be onto it in a flash, especially as he had a special 'thing' for Ben. Ben was good with all the kids, but with Billy he had established a one-to-one rapport over the months that the boy had spent on the ward.

It was ironic that Billy should still be here. Ben would be surprised to see him. By rights, he should have been having a spell at home right now, and only attending Outpatients for physio three times a week. He had been discharged a fortnight ago, but was back again following an accident.

True to his natural optimism, he had tried to walk unaided when his parents had taken their eyes off him for a moment, and he'd had a bad fall. By some miracle, he hadn't broken anything and there was no need for surgical intervention, but he'd badly pulled crucial ligaments in both knees which had had to be immobilised.

That meant another stay in hospital whilst his physiotherapy was reassessed and he started a programme of daily massage to keep his calf and foot muscles from deteriorating further. But he was still the same old Billy. With support extensions fitted to his wheelchair, he was still busying himself about the ward on his own and everyone else's business.

He came whizzing up now, as Holly was finishing her ten o'clock observations on the children she was specialling that day. His carroty hair looked spikier than usual—some spikes having elaborate twists to the ends.

Holly's gloomy thoughts lifted and she burst out laughing as he wheelied to a halt beside her. 'Billy, what *have* you been doing to your hair, and how on earth do you get those twists to stay put?'

'Soap,' said Billy succinctly, turning his head this way and that. 'I read about it in a mag. It's brill, isn't it?'

Holly shook her head in mock despair. 'As long as you don't go out in the rain,' she said, still laughing.

A young learner nurse doing her familiarisation stint

sped past with a bedpan on her way to the sluice. 'Like the hairdo, Billy,' she called over her shoulder. 'Just the job.'

Billy preened himself. 'Thanks, Carol. See, you shouldn't laugh at me, Nurse Holly,' he said reproachfully. 'Carol thinks it's great, and Dr Ben does too.'

'Oh, so you know he's back—you've seen him.'

Billy gave her a very straight, unblinking look from between his sandy eyelashes. 'Yeah…sure have, it's brill having him back, but…'

'But?' Holly prompted—might as well know the worst.

'He's kinda different, he looks…' He frowned and screwed up his face in an effort to explain what he meant. 'I dunno, sad, sort of…well, what I mean is, it's like part of him's missing…'

Part of him's missing! How apt. Of course it was. The twinkle in his startling green eyes; his bounce; his ability to laugh, to enjoy life and let it rub off on other people, especially the kids in his care.

Holly became aware that Billy was watching her, waiting for her to give him a lead. He needed an explanation as to why his idol, his chosen role model, wasn't his usual self. How much did Billy know about Ben's absence?

He'd asked plenty of questions before he'd gone home, and he must have heard some of the rumours that were rife. But how near were they to the truth? Because he was so bright and perceptive, it was easy to forget that he was only a child, and curious. Fond as he was of Ben, he might ask him awkward hurtful questions, unless he was put in the picture.

The sudden appearance of Ben at the top end of the ward made up her mind for her—she would have to be honest with Billy.

She said softly, 'Look, love, Dr Ben had a bad shock

when he was called away home a few weeks ago—that's why he's not quite himself, though he's come back to work. I'll explain later, but please don't say anything to him till I've done that.' She held out her hand palm upwards. 'Is it a deal?'

'Deal,' said Billy, with deadly seriousness clapping his hand down onto Holly's; then, with a knowing wink, he took himself off down the ward away from the approaching Ben.

Ben nodded Holly a greeting as he drew near. He was smiling slightly. 'Sealing a Billy-type deal, I see—care to share it with me?'

Holly shook her head and pursed her lips. 'More than my life's worth to do that. You know Billy—a deal's a deal.'

A flicker of amusement briefly wiped away the bleak expression. 'Hmm, know what you mean. His deals are famous—talk about an Englishman's word and all that. I must say it's good to see him. He's a sight for sore eyes, as Mrs Kelly would say.'

He laid his hand on Holly's arm and squeezed it in a familiar fashion. 'In fact it's great to be in harness again—brilliant—puts things in perspective, doing the job one was trained to do, being where one is needed.' He smiled—an unreal, mouth-only smile, Holly thought. 'And all thanks to you, love, not only beautiful but smart with it.'

His fingers tightened further, bit into the soft flesh of her forearm. A little trickle of alarm ran through her. He was almost too earnest, too intense and emphatic, almost as if he was trying to convince himself.

'Well,' she agreed in a calm voice, 'it certainly helps. But it's not the whole answer, Ben. Work for you and school for your Beth and James won't solve everything.

You must relax a bit—don't get so work focused that you've got no time left over for them. The kids here need you, but they need you too. It's good for them to get back into a routine, but that routine should include fun quality time with you.'

Ben stared at her. Slowly he released his hold on her arm. His mouth twisted into a parody of his crooked smile. '*Fun* time, *quality* time!' His voice was incredibly bitter, sarcastic. 'Even you, my dear Holly, can't work that miracle. That'll be up to Kirsty and Mrs Kelly to provide. I'll look after their trust fund, see that all their needs are provided for, but no way can I return to being the indulgent, carefree uncle ready for a quick romp. That character's gone for ever.'

Her voice low, conscious of nurses coming and going, the screech of children's voices and general background noises of the ward all around them, Holly said, 'Look, Ben, this isn't the time or place, but we should talk about this some more, that is…if you trust me enough to want to talk…'

Ben continued to stare stonily at her; then his shoulders sagged and his eyes filled with pain again and he murmured with infinite weariness, 'It's kind of you, Holly, but all the talk in the world won't bring my brother back to me, or restore to the kids their parents. I'm on my own. You pointed me in the right direction, but from now on it's down to me.'

Holly opened her mouth to speak; Ben shook his head and straightened his shoulders at the same time. 'No more talk, Holly, you get on and enjoy your life. You're funny, stunning, got everything going for you. When we first met, we were both footloose and fancy-free—you still are. We made a bargain, remember, no commitment. Don't saddle yourself with my problems.'

His square jaw set firmly, he straightened up some more, seeming to gain an inch or two, and said briskly, 'Now, I want to have a look at everybody, bring myself up to date. I've a lot of catching up to do. We'll start on the kids you're specialling.'

He was giving her the brush-off. He no longer wanted her help, was putting up barriers, barely seemed to want even her friendship. He had as good as said that... She was still footloose and fancy-free, and he wasn't, as if they were a different breed, belonged to different worlds.

Holly felt her chest muscles tighten with anger as she stared back at him. Did he really mean what he was saying, or was it grief talking? Did he really want her to move out of his personal life— carry on as if nothing had happened? Only days ago he had begged for her help based on a fragile, budding friendship—and she had given it. Now he was drawing a line under that brief episode as if it had never been.

He was already walking towards the next four-bedded bay. 'Well, come on, Nurse,' he said abruptly over his shoulder. 'Let's get on with it.'

Holly raised astonished eyebrows at his retreating back. This wasn't the Ben they all knew and loved, nor even the sad man who had joked with little Jessica Dench early that morning...this man was a stranger. And *something I said triggered off the change,* came the unpalatable thought as she followed the stranger into the bay. Perhaps talking about fun time with Beth and James *had* been pushing it a bit.

Ben had halted by the first bed and lifted the treatment chart from the foot rail. 'Hello, Tommy, I'm Dr Ben. How are you feeling today?'

He smiled his usual reassuring smile down at the small boy lying on top of the bed clothes. Tommy, dressed in shorts and a skimpy tee shirt and clutching a tattered-looking bunny rabbit to his chest, continued to stare fixedly up at the ceiling. There were bandages round his knees and elbows and a few reddened scaly lesions were visible on his thin torso where his tee shirt had ridden up.

On the point of losing her normal cool, Holly rushed into speech, keeping her voice low.

'Tommy has psoriasis, but there's also a query about his hearing, which seems to be intermittent. The ear consultant's due to see him this morning. Tommy's six. He was only admitted yesterday—he comes from a care home but they couldn't manage his psoriasis.'

Ben nodded, but said nothing.

His silence almost threw her, but she waded on. 'There are signs that it's beginning to clear up on much of his body, but his elbow and knee joints and scalp are still badly affected and very sore.'

A voice at the back of her head told her to pull herself together.

She went on softly, 'As to the deafness, they reckon he's only deaf when he wants to be, but I wouldn't like to comment on that. I haven't nursed him for long enough to pass an opinion.'

Ben nodded, but spoke this time, and, following Holly's lead, murmured with equal softness, 'Fair enough. I see he's on daily baths followed by an application of coal tar and salicyclic acid ointment to the psoriasis lesions.'

'Yes, ordered by Ken Wiseman when he saw him on admission. He plumped for conservative treatment. Tommy's had two treatments, one last night and one this morning.'

'Ken's a good senior house officer, I trust his judgement. We'll stick to that for the time being. Real or contrived, it's the deafness that bothers me more. Do we know any more of his history?'

'Only what I've told you. We don't even know why he's in care. The young assistant house father from the home, who brought him in, wasn't very forthcoming—I had the impression...' Holly's voice trailed off. She looked anxiously at Tommy who was still lying perfectly still.

Ben took her arm and edged her away from the foot of the bed. 'You had what impression?' His eyes bored into hers. 'Come on, Holly, give. This could be important; anything to do with a child's history is important. Don't hold back through a mistaken sense of protecting someone. Remember Birdy's maxim: kids first, last, and all the time.'

Holly met his eyes steadily. 'Of course you're right. Well, for what it's worth, I thought the chap who was with Tommy couldn't care less, couldn't wait to be shot of him. He intimated that Tommy was difficult and had been especially so since the psoriasis sprang up, following a chest infection. There is a note from the GP who attends the home, but it's very brief and to the point. It's in with his other notes—shall I fetch it?'

'No, I'll look at it when I've finished my round. Right now I'll see if I can get anything out of the lad.' He moved back into the cubicle and sat on the edge of the bed. 'Tommy, I'm going to examine you, but I won't disturb the bandages as Nurse Holly's given you a bath this morning. But I want to look at the scabby spots on your head and the rest of your body, and I also want to have a listen to your chest. OK?'

Tommy continued to look at the ceiling but his hands tightened round the battered bunny. He'd obviously heard what Ben had said.

'You can hold on to your bunny,' Ben added, 'but let Nurse pull your tee shirt up.'

Still clasping the tattered animal, Tommy lifted it up high.

'What's bunny's name?' Holly asked as she rolled up the little cotton shirt, repeating the question that she'd asked earlier when bathing him. Experience had taught her that speaking to or through a favourite toy often broke down barriers, though so far it hadn't worked with Tommy.

There was silence, then Tommy muttered almost inaudibly, 'Wilf,' and, lowering his arms, clasped the grubby, pathetic creature close to his bare chest. His eyes, full of tears, swivelled down from their study of the ceiling, and he raised his head with a jerk. 'Pl...please don't take him away.' He looked first at Ben and then at Holly.

Holly hissed in a painful breath and heard Ben smother an exclamation. She bent and kissed Tommy's forehead. 'Oh, love, of course we won't take him away. I think it's lovely to have something to cuddle. Tell you a secret—I take my teddy bear to bed with me every night. He's called Edward.'

In a strained voice Ben asked, 'Has anybody tried to take Wilf away from you, Tommy?'

There was another silence and the small chest moved up and down rapidly. Fear flickered in the tear-filled eyes that slid from side to side as he looked round the bay. He leaned forward till his head was almost touching both Holly's and Ben's.

'*He did,*' he whispered. 'The day I went to the home. He said big boys don't play with toys and he was going to make me grow up fast, but I hid Wilf till yesterday when they brought me here.'

'Who's ''he'', Tommy?'

'Darren.'

Darren rang a bell. 'Do you mean Darren Hooker, the man who brought you in yesterday?' Holly asked.

Tommy nodded. 'Don't tell him I said, he'll be ever so cross.'

Holly looked at Ben over the boy's head. He was looking grim. 'It's all right, son,' he said softly. 'We won't tell Darren anything, but there's something else you can tell me—were any of the other boys frightened of Darren?'

'Yes, one boy tried to run away but they caught him and brought him back, but that was before I went to the home.'

Twenty minutes later when he had finished checking Tommy and the other boys in the bay, Ben burst out furiously, 'I'll nail that man for this. What the hell's he doing working in a care home? Some house father. Fancy scaring a little kid like that—threatening to take away his only bit of comfort—I wonder what other kids he's frightened to death? No wonder Tommy plays hard of hearing, it's his only refuge.'

Holly had never seen him so angry, and she too was smouldering, but trying to hold her temper down.

'Do you want to cancel the ear man who's coming to see him?'

'No!' He was emphatic. 'I want it to be known that his hearing may be disturbed for psychological, rather than physiological or anatomical reasons…if that is the case.' He balled one fist and clapped it into the palm of his other hand. 'My God, I'm going to get to the bottom of this. Mr Darren Hooker won't know what hit him, nor will the senior house father, who, if he doesn't, should know what's going on.'

He began to stalk up the ward towards the station.

Holly had almost to run to keep up with him, whilst trying to keep her cool. Warning bells were clanging in her head. She must get Ben to calm down. Supposing they were barking up the wrong tree? Supposing little Tommy was exaggerating or had misunderstood the man Darren?

OK, she hadn't liked what she'd seen of him, but maybe Tommy was a difficult child—not all kids, even sick ones, were angels. Ben would look all kinds of a fool if it turned out that the boy was a disruptive influence in the care home, and they only had his word for it that Darren had threatened to take his cuddly toy away from him.

She recalled the fear in Tommy's eyes, his hands clutching Wilf to his chest, and knew that he wasn't play-acting, the threat had been real enough. But she must still try to get Ben to calm down and look at the situation rationally, not go in with all guns blazing on his own. The hospital social worker would have to be involved and make contact with the home. It would then be up to the home administrator to sort the matter out.

'No,' said Ben forcefully, when they reached the station and she put this to him. 'I'm going to do this direct. Any action they may take will take for ever. And, according to Tommy, at least one kid has tried to run away. Small kids don't do that for nothing.'

His eyes were sparkling with rage. 'Meanwhile, this man will go on terrifying the vulnerable children in his care. It could be happening right now and I'm going to put a stop to it. May I have Tommy's notes, please? I've a phone call to make to whoever's in charge of this home, and I'll do it from my office.'

Holly found the notes and handed them over. She made one more attempt to cool things. 'Let's talk it through,' she suggested. 'Marshall our facts—we don't want to go off half cock.'

'My facts are marshalled,' said Ben. 'We have one scared child suffering from psoriasis, probably brought about by a viral infection, but almost certainly aggravated by general debility caused by acute fear and unhappiness. And, as far as we know, at least one other child has suffered enough to try to make a run for it. There's something rotten going on in this home, Holly, and I mean to get to the bottom of it.'

For the second time that morning he walked away from her, his back stiff and uncompromising...the back of a lonely man going into battle.

Holly stared at his retreating back. She couldn't let him do this on his own. She raced after him and caught up with him just outside the ward. She put a hand on his forearm and felt the strong muscles tense beneath the silky scattering of hairs.

He turned to face her, his eyes clashing with hers.

'You're not going to stop me, Holly, that man shouldn't be working with children. He may not be beating kids up physically, but by God he's damaging them emotionally, to say the least, and nobody appears to be doing anything about it—it may even be the tip of an iceberg of—at best indifference, at worst...'

Holly met his stormy eyes steadily. 'Ben, I don't want to stop you. You can count on me to back you up when the authorities get involved, and they will. They'll be on the defensive they always are when their authority is questioned. They'll be furious with you for not going through the proper channels and might even try to block you.'

She squeezed his arm fiercely, as he had squeezed hers a short while ago, and in a low, husky, earnest voice, said, 'Ben, I'm with you all the way. I just want you to know that you're not on your own,' and, standing on tiptoe, she reached up and kissed his cheek.

Ben looked startled for an instant, then grabbed her hands and brought them to his lips. 'Thanks, Holly Brown,' he murmured, 'for coming to my rescue yet again.'

Then with a nod, and a crooked smile, he turned and walked off down the corridor. But this time, Holly fancied, his back didn't look quite so lonely.

CHAPTER FIVE

HOLLY decided that she would open a bottle of wine and sit down and do some hard thinking that evening when she got back to her flat. After the day's events, she had a lot of unresolved problems to sort out—most of them to do with Ben.

With the exception of catching a fleeting glimpse of him with the ear consultant when he'd visited Tommy Warner, she hadn't seen anything of him after he'd stalked off to make his phone call. Both the surgical and the medical units had been breathlessly busy with discharges and admissions and the odd emergency, and her feet had hardly touched the ground.

At five o'clock, at the tail-end of her duty period, Billy Bowman buttonholed her, reminding her that she had promised to fill him in on the reasons for Ben's withdrawal symptoms that he'd so graphically described that morning.

Billy led her into the play room at the end of the ward, which was suspiciously empty.

'What did you do with the other kids, Billy, magic them away?' Holly asked, folding herself down onto one of the low chairs.

Billy grinned. 'Something like that,' he said, and tapped his nose in a sort of parody of a wise old man. In fact, thought Holly, watching him settle himself back in his elongated wheelchair, arms folded across his chest, spiky head tilted at a listening angle, he looked a bit like a wise old man waiting to hear what she had to say—and, God help her, she had better get it right.

She reminded herself that Billy was eight, going on nine, and not ninety. She cleared her throat.

Billy's grin faded. 'I thought it would be better if we had a bit of hush so you can give me the low-down on Dr Ben.'

The low-down! There wasn't any way to wrap it up, so she stuck to the facts of the accident, but left out the harrowing bits about the identification process, though she was aware that it was that which had so largely contributed to the shock factor and Ben's state of mind. She then went on to explain that Ben had been left to care for his small niece and nephew, who had lost their parents.

'So you see,' she wound up, 'it's not surprising that Dr Ben's not his usual self. He's got a lot on his mind, and it was a dreadful shock losing his twin brother; they were very close friends as well as being brothers.'

Sharp, intelligent eyes wide, Billy stared at her for a moment in silence, then unerringly homed in on the salient points.

'Gruesome,' he said. Gruesome was an 'in' word with the children at present. 'Twins are special, aren't they? My mum's a twin, and she told me once that my Aunty Tina was like—well—part of herself. Do you think that's how Dr Ben felt about his brother?'

'That's exactly how he felt…still feels—he's absolutely gutted about his brother's death.'

'And those kids that he's looking after, are they little?'

'Beth is six and James four.'

Billy unfolded and refolded his arms, hugging himself tight. He made a whistling sound through his teeth. 'Poor little kids,' he muttered. 'Dunno how I'd feel if I lost my mum and dad.' He blinked and his eyes glistened.

He's incredible, thought Holly. How many other eight-year-olds would make that sort of connection and be so sorry for children they didn't know. But that was Billy.

She said softly, 'Well, that's not going to happen, Billy. Your mum and dad are going to come breezing in tomorrow just as usual, and, as for Beth and James, they've got their Uncle Ben to take care of them.'

'Yeah.' Billy brightened. 'I bet he's brilliant at that. So what can I do to make him feel better about things, Nurse Holly?'

Holly had a sudden inspiration. 'You can go and chat up Tommy Warner, the boy who came in yesterday. Dr Ben's worried about him. I know he'd be pleased if you made a mate of him. Only take it easy, he's had a bit of a fright recently.'

Billy unfolded his arms and nodded. 'Righty-o, will do.' He wheeled himself round to face the door and beamed a sideways smile at Holly. 'Thanks for telling me about the Doc, Nurse. I'm glad you're his friend, he's a very special sort of guy.'

It takes one to know one, thought Holly, a while later, back in her flat reviewing her conversation with Billy. Talk about an old head on young shoulders, as Granny would say. Billy certainly is one in a million. She congratulated herself on suggesting that he made friendly overtures to Tommy. He was exactly the sort of person the younger boy needed as friend and champion, and, as a plus, Billy would feel that he was doing something positive for Ben.

And Ben would approve, be relieved that Billy had taken Tommy under his wing. It would be of some comfort to him. Clearly the boy's condition had shaken him to the core and had raised in him all his protective instincts. Clearly, too, he was deeply concerned for the other children in the home.

On the face of it, perhaps depriving a small boy of a favourite toy was not an enormous crime in itself, but to a sensitive man like Ben it signified a subtle cruelty that must be stamped out. He was dead right—a man who could do that could do anything and shouldn't be working with children, especially with vulnerable children already deprived of so much.

Ben was right too in thinking that the administration of the home was slack, perhaps worse than slack, if they employed someone like the awful Darren. Surely someone senior must have noticed his attitude to the children. Noticed and not said anything—not cared! Not dared!

Holly took a long, thoughtful sip of wine. Although she had offered her support to Ben when he'd gone off to make the phone call that was likely to stir up a hornets' nest, she had not been entirely convinced that this was the best way to deal with the matter. Left to herself she would have gone through the proper channels—and the matter might have hung fire for weeks, perhaps months, she acknowledged wryly, and in that time…

Her mobile buzzed making her jump, slopping a little red wine onto her uniform tunic and trousers. 'Damn, damn, damn,' she muttered as she switched on the receiver.

'Sorry, obviously bad timing,' said Ben's voice in her ear. 'Am I interrupting anything?'

Her heart missed a beat. 'No,' she said in a voice as neutral as his, though her mind went into overdrive. Why was he ringing? Was he still upset? What had been the result of his telephone conversation with the administrator of the home? His voice gave nothing away.

How should she respond if he did want to involve her since earlier he had given her the brush-off?

'Holly, you were right yet again about talking—my head's full to bursting. I'm off in twenty minutes. Could you bear to meet me and let me unload?'

Could she? Did she have a choice? 'You can come over to the flat when you're free.' She kept her voice cool. 'I'm now stocked up and can offer you something stronger than tea or coffee.'

There was a pause. 'I'd rather not, too many prying eyes. Could it be somewhere neutral? I'll meet you outside the entrance. I belong to a club within walking distance and it's a nice night for walking.'

Holly looked out of the window. The myriad lights of the hospital, across the square separating it from the residents' home, glowed against the darkening sky. The sun had just set on a showery, windy April day. The wind had fallen. It was a nice night, though, unlike in Shropshire soon after dusk where a few muted stars would be twinkling, there were no stars visible. She missed the stars.

'Do you know every pub and club within a ten mile radius of Lizzie's?'

He almost chuckled. 'Ninety per cent, I should think…legacy of my free and easy past.'

He was making an effort to lighten up. Would it help him if she agreed to a meeting and let him unload?

She had warned him against bottling things up a few days ago. It had been good advice; she'd better stick to it.

'OK, I'll meet you outside in half an hour.

Ben was waiting for her, prowling up and down between the ambulance bay for A and E and the main entrance.

He greeted her rather curtly, then took her elbow and

steered her out between the parked BMWs and Bentleys belonging to the consultants, into a narrow street down which she hadn't yet ventured. In fact it was little more than a feebly lit cobbled alleyway between high-walled gardens of towering Victorian houses. Jack the Ripper land, thought Holly, and shivered.

'Cold?' asked Ben in a surprised voice.

'No—this alleyway, it's a bit scary, full of history, full of ghosts of things past, yet we're only a few minutes away from the hospital and bright lights.'

Ben released her elbow and took her hand and gave it a squeeze. The pressure of his fingers was warm and comforting. 'That's London for you, full of these little backwaters. But I wouldn't have thought that you scared that easily, you're usually so damned breezy and sure of yourself—it's almost a relief to find that Staff Nurse Holly Brown can be ruffled.'

Holly stopped abruptly and turned to face him. 'You make me sound…superficial,' she said.

Ben looked surprised. In the dim light his eyes were just dark pools; they could have been any colour. His hands came up and rested on her shoulders. He brought his face, smelling faintly of musk and antiseptic, close to hers, and enunciated slowly and earnestly, 'Holly, if it hadn't been for you I'd have cracked up completely. You've not only saved me from going round the twist, but Beth and James too—you were so right about them going back to school. And, far from being superficial, you are the toughest, strongest person I know, full of hidden depths. Being breezy is all part of that, being scared of a dark alley way is simply endearing—does wonders for my male ego—the flaw that stops you being too perfect.'

'Oh,' said Holly, shaken, feeling her cheeks burn at the heaped compliments. She rallied and chuckled. 'Oh, believe me, I've plenty of flaws, but I'm glad to have bolstered up your ego. Fragile things, male egos.'

'That's true,' said Ben softly, 'and mine's particularly fragile at present. It can do with all the bolstering you can provide.' He leaned forward and pressed his lips to her cheek. 'You know, love, today's been full of highs and lows. Fool that I am, I was so sure at one point that I could manage on my own—submerge myself in work—but I can't, Holly. I need your particular brand of help and common sense, but…'

'But…' She peered up at him in the dim lamplight. What did he have doubts about? Her willingness? He shouldn't have; she'd made it plain enough surely that she wanted to help him and his small niece and nephew. Or did he think that she had some ulterior motive, like trying to use the situation as a foundation for more than friendship?

Well, he shouldn't have doubts about that either, since on their first date she'd made it plain that she hadn't been looking for commitment or a long-term relationship. She still wasn't. What she wanted was his friendship, earning her the right to offer help, for, although she was on good terms with her colleagues, and particularly with Jan, she still often felt alone in the big city away from her home and family.

She repeated, 'But?'

Ben's hands gripped her shoulders. 'But I don't want you to feel…trapped.'

'Trapped? Why should I feel trapped, Ben?'

Taking her by surprise, he ran the fingers of one hand through her crisp tawny hair that covered her scalp like a neat shiny cap—it was an intimate, tender gesture.

'It suits you so well,' he murmured. 'Mostly I go for

long hair but this is all part of you, Holly, totally in character…'

'You haven't told me why I might feel trapped, Ben.'

'It'll keep till we get to the club.'

He took her hand again and they walked to the end of the alley which opened onto a wide, well-lit busy street. They turned right past a delicatessen, a boutique, a betting shop and a hairdresser's, and then into a narrower street of tall, elegant buildings with railed basements and railed steps leading up to solid, shiny front doors with brass knockers.

The sort, thought Holly, her head full of colourful musicals, that would be opened by staid-looking butlers or footmen in knee breeches.

No butler or footman opened the door of number five. Ben simply turned the polished fluted knob and, pushing the door open, ushered her into a bright, beautifully proportioned hall, lit by a gleaming chandelier.

'Welcome to the forties club,' he said, and then, nodding towards a man behind a highly polished mahogany reception desk, 'Evening, Trevor. This is Miss Brown. We're signing in for dinner.'

'Evening, sir—miss.'

Holly returned a polite greeting to Trevor, but frowned at Ben. Signing in for dinner—it sounded very formal, a bit daunting. Everything was a bit daunting: the building, the club, the respectful Trevor in his bow-tie and striped waistcoat, not a bit what she'd expected. But then nothing to do with Ben was what she had expected when she'd first met him.

She murmured, 'You asked me to have a drink and a chat, not a three-course meal.'

'We can make it two courses, or even one, or have a snack in the buttery. You haven't eaten, have you?'

'No, but…' It was on the tip of her tongue to suggest that they kept their chat brief and then he should go home to Beth and James. Instinct warned her that this wouldn't be a good move; she'd rattled him this morning with her references to the children and his responsibilities to them, and touched a raw spot which had made him clam up on her. She mustn't risk this happening a second time—she must just let him go at his own pace. 'OK, the buttery, then—whatever that is.'

The serve-yourself buttery was in the basement. It had its own miniature drinks bar presided over by a pretty barmaid, whom Ben introduced as Maeve. The buttery was a good choice for a quiet chat. Except for a party of six smartly dressed men and women who looked as if they were snacking before going on to the theatre or cinema, the long room, comfortably furnished with squashy sofas, easy chairs and low tables, was empty.

A couple of people in the party group lifted their hands and nodded to Ben as he and Holly waited for their drinks at the bar.

'Friends of yours?' asked Holly as Ben returned the salute.

'Sort of. Fellow members of the club,' Ben replied. 'Known them for years.'

Maeve set their drinks down on the bar. Ben didn't pay for them, but signed a docket presented to him by Maeve.

Holly was intrigued. 'Is this a private club?' she asked as they moved over to the buffet laid out on a long refectory table.

Ben nodded. 'Founded in the nineteen forties by service men and women. One has to be sponsored for membership. It's a bit like getting into Eton.'

She was further intrigued. 'So who sponsored you for membership?'

'A great-uncle—he was a pilot in the air force during the war. He only died a few years ago in his eighties. He sponsored both me and Josh for membership when we were born.' He gave her a wry smile. 'I told you it was rather like getting into a top public school.'

It was another little interesting piece in the patchwork of his history and something that might bring them closer.

'My grandfather was in the air force too during the war,' she said. 'I used to love hearing all about the Battle of Britain and dogfights over the Channel, when I was a kid. It was like one of those old war movies.'

Ben's eyes met hers. Briefly they looked warm, alive, brighter, and some of the strain had gone out of them. He said softly, 'Uncle Marcus was choc-full of stories too and we loved them. What a lot we have in common—no wonder that we hit it off right from the start.' He pushed his drink into her hand. 'Look, you go and sit down and I'll see to the food. Anything you'd like particularly?'

Holly looked at the long table laden with multi-coloured tossed salads and cold meats and pickles. 'Mmm, talk about spoiled for choice. I'll have the salmon and as much salad as you can cram on the plate, please…oh, and some garlic bread.'

Pleased by his words and the expression in his eyes, and the fact that they had the air force in common, she suddenly felt more relaxed, less overawed by her surroundings or the well dressed crowd across the room—and realised how hungry she was.

She made her way over to a low table with two armchairs ranged opposite each other, and, when Ben arrived a couple of minutes later with piled-up plates, attacked her food ravenously.

After swallowing a few forkfuls, she paused to sip at her dry Martini. 'Sorry about scoffing like that but I missed coffee, lunch and a tea break,' she said apologetically. 'It's been that sort of day.'

'Don't be sorry,' said Ben. 'Like I told you once before, it's refreshing to see a woman enjoying her food.'

Holly was surprised and rather touched that, after all that had happened, he remembered anything about their first date.

'I bet you missed out on meals too, but you're not doing much about it.' She nodded towards his almost untouched food.

He made a stab at a piece of chicken and examined it on the end of his fork. 'Yep, you're right, I'm hungry but, for the first time ever, I've felt lately that food would choke me.' He popped the chicken into his mouth, chewed and swallowed, obviously without much enjoyment. 'I can't seem to straighten myself out, Holly.' His hands tightened round his knife and fork till the knuckles whitened.

'When I first came on duty this morning, I felt quite exhilarated and as if I was coming through this awful fog of pain of losing Josh, and then everything suddenly fell apart again when I realised that I was just being thoroughly selfish.'

'Because of what I said about fun time with Beth and James,' Holly muttered. 'Me and my big mouth.'

Ben shook his head. 'No, Holly, you and your wise mouth. You were spot on. I just couldn't—or didn't want to—take it on board, but seeing little Tommy Warner put things back in perspective. I wonder if that little chap's had any fun time in his life? Somehow I doubt it.'

Holly stretched her hands out across the table and stroked his white knuckles. 'He has some happy memories,' she said softly. 'Wilf, for instance.'

'A tattered bunny falling to pieces.'

'But like the crown jewels to him. And you've be-friended him, taken up the cudgels on his behalf—like everything else, happiness is relative. I would say at this moment he is sound asleep clutching Wilf to his skinny little chest and feeling happier and safer than he has for yonks after a visit from our Billy.' She didn't wait for his reaction but asked, 'By the way, what sort of response did you get from the home administrator?'

'As you might expect—cold, defensive, but I left him in no doubt that I wasn't going to let this drop.' He frowned. 'What do you mean, a visit from Billy?'

Holly explained about Billy and how he had cornered her.

Ben looked incredulous. 'Do you mean that he was con-cerned about me, saw through my clowning around?'

'He did, and desperately wanted to do something to cheer you up. Knowing how bothered you were about Tommy, knowing what a shot in the arm Billy can be, it seemed a good idea to point him in Tommy's direction.'

Ben's face lit up. 'It was little short of brilliant,' he said.

Holly chuckled. 'Just me being my practical self. In fact I think I'll tackle Birdy about moving Tommy into Billy's bay—they'd be good for each other.' She took another mouthful of Martini and eyed Ben over the rim of her glass. 'OK, Ben, now come clean. What did you mean earlier about you making me feel trapped? It sounded rather dramatic.'

He looked surprised by her sudden change of direction, but didn't try to evade her question. He put down his knife and fork, and, resting his elbows on the arms of his chair, linked his fingers beneath his chin.

'Dramatic, perhaps, but with some reason. You've al-ready given me help more than I deserved considering our short friendship, and I'm going to ask you for more, Holly—more for the children's sake than for mine. I want you to meet them.'

He unclasped and then re-clasped his hands beneath his chin.

Holly was conscious of a trickle of excitement running up and down her spine. He wanted her to meet Beth and James—great! But why was he making such a meal of it? She took another sip of her drink. Why should she mind meeting the children?

She said softly, 'I should like to meet them, Ben. I don't see any problems there.'

He took in a deep breath. 'I need someone to guide me, hold my hand, remind me where the priorities are—like you did this morning.'

Holly nodded. 'That's what friends are for.'

Ben put a finger to her lips. 'But,' he said firmly, 'before you agree, I want you to know that I'm not asking you to be a substitute mum and be around all the time; you must do your own thing, go out and about. Like I said, you're footloose and—'

'Fancy-free, I think were the words you used,' broke in Holly, 'as we both were when we first met. We also said then, Ben, no strings attached. OK, if that's what you want, we can approach this in the same way. But you also said on our first date that you wanted to lay the foundations of a firm friendship—and what are friends for but to be around when most needed?'

Ben dropped his finger from her lips, and gazed in fascination into her lovely blue eyes flashing fire. He leaned across the low table and cupped her flushed cheeks and firm jaw in his strong hands.

In a voice touched with humour reminiscent of the old Ben, he murmured, 'Do I take that as a yes?'

'Definitely,' said Holly.

CHAPTER SIX

SISTER BIRDY didn't need any persuading to move Tommy Warner into Billy's bay.

'Sounds sensible enough,' she said, after Holly had given her a brief outline of the little boy's unhappy experiences.

Holly played down Ben's reaction to the situation, saying simply that he'd made contact with the home. She still felt uneasy about the way he had handled the matter by going over the heads of the hospital brass. She just prayed that it wouldn't backfire on him…and possibly on her for supporting him—not that she would backtrack; she'd given her word.

She wasn't quite sure how her superior might react. For Sister Birdy, though a law unto herself where her young patients were concerned, might not approve of him taking such independent action. But she might have known that the old warrior of a ward sister would be on the side of whom she considered the righteous—in this case her precious children. Her first words after agreeing to the bed switch, were: 'Well, well, so Ben's already had a word with the home's administrator, Holly, is that what you're telling me?'

Put like that, it sounded almost innocuous. What, of course, Sister didn't know was how blazingly angry he'd been when he'd made the call and what he might have said.

Holly nodded. 'He felt that the sooner the powers that be were put in the picture, the better.' She took a deep

breath. You stood by your friends. 'And I agree with him.'
She knew that she sounded defiant. In for a penny, in for
a pound, she thought.

'*Good,*' Sister Birdy said emphatically. 'Leave it to the
top bods and it could be years before anything was done
about the situation, by which time…'

Holly exhaled noisily. 'Phew, I thought you might be
mad, Sister, as we didn't go through the usual channels.'

The blackbird-like eyes twinkled. 'Did you, now? I'll
let you into a secret, Nurse: my maternal grandmother was
a suffragette. If she and other like-minded women had
gone through the usual channels—I doubt women would
have had the vote yet. Think on that, my dear. Sometimes
the rules have to be bent, sometimes—' She broke off to
look past Holly and smile.

Holly turned to see Ben standing in the doorway. He
looked, she thought, tired, but in a curious way—elated,
less gaunt than in the last week or so since he'd made
contact. Was it due to their conversation of last night and
the warm kiss that they had exchanged when parting?

'To seal our pact of friendship,' he'd said, holding her
close so that their bodies had melded into each other. And,
fleetingly, his hazel-green eyes had smiled down into hers.

Whatever the reason, it was good to see him looking
less haunted.

Sister Birdy said cheerfully, 'Come in, Ben—Nurse
Holly and I were having a chat about cutting through red
tape. I understand that, re Tommy Warner, you've had the
scissors out already.'

Ben smiled. 'You approve! Knew I could depend on
you, Birdy, thanks. But I think we should keep your support between the three of us.' He turned and smiled at
Holly. 'Don't go spreading it around, Holly.'

Birdy chuckled. 'Ah, the white knight protecting his

loyal followers from the overlords. You know, there's no need on my account—I've got a certain amount of clout in this place and have had a good few run-ins over the years with management—but I agree that Holly must keep a low profile—'

'But I don't want to,' Holly interrupted. 'I wasn't sure if Ben was right, but I am now, and I think the people at the top should get their fingers out and investigate what's going on in that home.' She felt her cheeks flush and tilted her head defiantly. 'I know I'm only small fry, but...'

'It's because you're small fry in the hospital hierarchy that you need protecting,' said Birdy. 'I know it's not fair, but that's the way the cookie crumbles. You can't afford to pick up any black marks—your time will come. It's one of the perks of age and experience to say what you think, but until then keep a still tongue. Think dire thoughts but don't express them.'

She looked at her watch. 'Don't spoil your copy book. Lizzie's needs nurses like you, the kids need you, and, as a matter of fact, they need you right now. So off you go and organise Tommy's move.' She waved a hand in dismissal. The expression on her face said, No argument.

Holly knew when she was beaten. She shrugged. 'I'm on my way, Sister.'

Ben said softly as she slipped past him, 'See you at lunch-time—half one if you can make it.'

Back in the ward, Holly found Carol Smith, the learner observer, tidying the counter at the nurses' station, obviously at a loose end.

'Would you like to come with me and help do a bed switch?'
she asked.

Carol's eyes lit up. 'Please, Staff, I'm bored out of my

skull. No one seems to want me this morning, yet everyone is *so* busy.'

'I sympathise,' said Holly. 'It can all seem pretty aimless till you get hooked in on your speciality. Everyone but you seems to know what they're about. Anyway, let's get cracking and move Tommy Warner into Billy Bowman's bay. We'll shift the empty bed in there to Tommy's space, ready for the new patient due in later today.'

'Why don't we just put the new patient in the empty bed? It would save time.'

They were walking swiftly up the ward and Holly slowed to a halt. She laid a hand on the young girl's arm. 'Saving time isn't always a priority,' she said. 'The priority is the patient's need—in this case, Tommy's.'

Carol frowned. 'I don't understand. We can treat him just as well where he is, can't we? Give him his bath and put that yucky ointment on his spots?'

'We can physically treat his psoriasis in any bed—but that's almost the least of Tommy's problems, and hopefully we can clear it up in a short while.'

'So...' Carol raised puzzled eyebrows.

'Tommy's a frightened, withdrawn little boy. He comes from a children's home and needs a friend. We think Billy will be a good friend to him—and that's what he needs, a good friend. I know it's not easy to understand. Physical wounds can be seen, emotional ones can't—can you appreciate that?'

Carol's pert little face with its fringe of curly hair hardened—she suddenly looked years older than her teenage years, and her voice too was hard when she spoke. 'Should do,' she said through tight lips. 'I was in a kids' home. I was there till I was ten, and then I was adopted.'

Her hard little face softened. 'It was the most brilliant

day of my life. Oh, don't get me wrong,' she added when she saw Holly's horrified expression. 'They were all right in the home, I wasn't badly treated or anything...' she heaved in a deep breath. '...but there was no one for me, specifically. I was one of a crowd.'

Incredibly touched at the thought of a lonely little girl longing for a mother's exclusive love, Holly said gently, 'Oh, Carol, how horrible. I can't imagine... Is that why you wanted to try out paediatric nursing—so that you could care for children?'

'Partly, and partly because my adoptive mum was a children's nurse and she's the tops—I'd just like to be like her.'

'Well, there's absolutely no reason why you shouldn't be.' Holly made her voice brisk, though she felt like marshmallow inside. 'I've been keeping an eye on you, and I think you've got what it takes to be a good nurse—and your background will be an asset. Now, love, we'd better get moving and do this bed change.'

She kept Carol with her for the rest of the morning after they had moved Tommy in with Billy. Holly was determined to nurture a likely future paediatric nurse who appeared to have all the right qualities.

'We're going to renew the dressings to Marianne Watson's feet and her toes in particular,' she explained in a low voice as they entered a four-bedded bay. 'Marianne's twelve and has Raynaud's Disease. It's a painful circulatory condition, which cuts off or decreases the blood supply to many parts of the body. The limbs and extremities, fingers and toes, are most often affected, producing ulcers which can turn gangrenous, unless they are kept scrupulously clean and circulation is gently improved.'

Carol's eyes widened. 'What happens if they turn gangrenous? That means dead, doesn't it?' She shuddered.

'Yep. In extreme cases a finger or toe or a larger limb has to be amputated, but medication to improve the circulation is getting more efficient and sophisticated—and herbal medicines are often found to be effective, and are now being taken into account and administered with, or in place of, conventional drugs. Also, physiotherapy, massage and swimming help.

'That's why Marianne's here. Most of the time she can be managed at home. Her parents are sensible people who make sure she's well wrapped up and doesn't go out when the weather's too cold or wet. Not much fun for a lively twelve-year-old, but Marianne is usually co-operative. Unfortunately, she recently went to stay with a friend for a couple of days and got her feet wet. No big deal for a normal kid but serious for Marianne.

'She didn't like to make a fuss at her friend's house and kept her wet shoes on for hours, resulting in ulcerated toes on both feet, and on one foot, the heel as well.' She looked hard at Carol—she was very young. 'Changing the dressings isn't exactly a picnic for Marianne—perhaps you would rather go and chat up one of the other girls while I'm doing them.'

'No way, Staff, I'm not that much of a wimp. It's the sort of thing I'll have to get used to, isn't it, if I'm to follow in my mum's footsteps?'

Holly beamed at her. 'That's my girl,' she said. She started to push the dressings trolley towards the corner bed. 'Come on, then, let's get stuck in.'

Marianne was lying in bed with her sheets and blankets pulled up to her chin. A bed cradle lifted the clothes from her feet and legs. Her eyes were closed and the radio headset was clamped round her ears.

Holly touched her shoulder gently and Marianne opened her eyes—and then quickly squeezed them shut. 'Oh, no, not you,' she groaned, and flicked open her eyes again.

Holly cocked her head on one side. 'Well, there's a nice greeting. Look, love, do you mind if Carol gives me a hand? She's not seen this procedure before.'

Marianne's eyebrows shot up and in an incredulous voice, she said, 'You mean you *want* to see my gruesome toes?'

Carol nodded. 'That's right,' she replied.

'Weird,' said Marianne, and then, 'Why?'

'Because I want to be a nurse like Staff here or my mum—she was a nurse.'

'Like your mum?' Marianne sounded astonished. 'Weird,' she repeated. 'I wouldn't like to be a hairdresser like my mum.'

Perhaps you would if you'd not had one all your life, thought Holly. She rolled the bedclothes back over the cradle, lifted it off the bed and began to unwrap the bandages from Marianne's feet.

Carol was watching what she was doing, but asked Marianne, 'What do you want to be when you leave school or university?'

Marianne hissed in a breath when Holly finished removing the outer bandages and began soaking off the dressings stuck to individual toes, but she was diverted by Carol's question.

'I want to be a dancer,' she said. She looked from Holly to Carol, and tossed her head. 'Oh, I know you think I can't be because of these—'she pointed to her feet '—but they've never been bad like this before and I've been going to dancing lessons since I was little. I'll be able to start again when they get better.'

A dancer of all things—why not something more secure?

Holly began swabbing the raw, ulcerated toes. 'We use a mild antiseptic solution for this,' she explained to Carol, 'and then a healing ointment made especially for Marianne in our laboratory.' Carefully she applied gauze squares spread with the ointment to each toe and the heel of the right foot. 'How's that?' she asked.

'Brilliant, I hardly felt anything this morning.' Marianne was looking at Carol. 'Bet you think I'm crazy wanting to dance?'

'No,' said Carol. 'Not if you want it hard enough.' Her cheeks flushed slightly. 'I wanted something hard once, and I got it.' She flashed a conspiratorial glance at Holly.

She means she wanted a loving mum, Holly realised, and felt privileged to be in the young girl's confidence.

After a busy morning, she sent Carol to an early lunch. 'Thanks for your help,' she told her. 'You've done brilliantly, especially with Marianne.'

'Would it help if I talked to her sometimes?' Carol asked. 'I'm here for another week.'

'It would help tremendously. Nursing's all about talking and listening, not just giving injections and medicines—the whole person needs caring for.' Holly laid a restraining hand on the girl's arm. 'And, Carol, don't lose touch. Come and see us when you get back to university. We'll always be glad to see you and there are always kids who don't have many visitors—they could do with a one to one.'

Carol's heart-shaped face lit up. 'I'd like that,' she said, almost dancing out of the ward.

Holly went off to supervise lunches.

Supervising lunches by senior staff was a must with Sister Birdy. 'It's a nurses' job,' she would tell new staff on the ward, 'to check what the children eat, and not to be left to the catering staff. I'm not talking special diets, that goes without saying, but you can tell a lot about a child's progress by the way he or she tackles their food. Anything out of the ordinary and I want to hear about it pronto.'

Holly let her mind wander to Ben whilst she was supervising. She'd only caught fleeting glimpses of him during the morning as he'd flitted between the surgical and medical sides of the unit. He'd looked relaxed and almost happy when she'd seen him in Sister's office that morning. Long may it last, she prayed.

At one-thirty there was only a scattering of people in the large cafeteria: a few staff and a handful of patients' visitors. Ben signalled to her from across the room. I've got yours, he mouthed, pointing to the table.

Holly could see two trays set down opposite each other. Her first thought was, How sweet, her second, But a bit high-handed—how on earth does he know what I fancy?

In fact it was exactly what she fancied: an egg mayonnaise and cheese sandwich, fresh fruit salad and cream, and a steaming cup of coffee.

'I owe you,' she said with a smile as she sat down.

'On the contrary.' His eyes met hers. 'I owe you more than I can ever repay.'

'Friends don't want repaying.' She bit into her sandwich. 'Mmm, this is yummy, I'm…'

His eyes actually twinkled. 'Starving,' he suggested.

'Got it in one.' She studied his face. It definitely looked less lined, less haggard, more rounded. He was almost like the carefree man she'd met on that first date.

Almost! His eyes had twinkled briefly and some of the lines scored down his cheeks and round his mouth, that he'd acquired since his brother's death, had softened. But she was conscious that much of the time he was putting on an act—a brave front, her mother would call it. Watching him as he bit into his own sandwich, Holly thought, It's going to be a long haul getting him back to normal—hope I'm up to it.

They ate in silence for a few minutes—at least he'd got something of an appetite today—then Ben put the remains of his sandwich on the plate and wiped his mouth with his napkin.

'Have you thought about what I suggested for tonight?' he asked.

Holly nodded. 'Yes, but I'm still not sure whether it's a bit too soon for the children to meet a stranger, and Kirsty may feel that I'm muscling in on her territory, and I wouldn't blame her if she did.'

'You won't be like a stranger. I talked to James and Beth before they went to school this morning—in fact I took them to school which is why I was a bit late in. I told them all about you, explained that we were friends and worked together, and that you wanted to meet them.'

'And Kirsty?'

'She thought it was a brilliant idea. In fact I think she's quite looking forward to meeting another woman near her own age. Mrs Kelly's a dear, but old enough to be her granny. She misses Anthea's company dreadfully, they were friends as well as employer and employee.' His eyes pleaded with her. 'Please come, we all want you to.'

Holly was suddenly conscious that his foot was touching hers. He was stroking his toe along the outer border of her foot and even through the leather of their shoes it felt provocative—sensual—or was this her imagination at work?

Perhaps the touch was accidental—or perhaps this was

a sign that the old flirtatious Ben was returning, however slowly.

His eyes continued to plead. There was no hint of the frivolous Ben. 'Convinced?'

Holly drew her feet back under her chair. Damn her vivid imagination. She smiled. 'Convinced! Am I? Yes, probably. You've certainly done your groundwork.'

He breathed a sigh of what she presumed was relief. 'You're off at three; I'll meet you in Reception at four. We'll take a taxi and be home in time for nursery tea, and you can help me tuck the kids into bed and read them a story. I'll be on call this evening, but with luck there won't be any emergencies which the team can't handle.'

'You're very determined about this.'

'That's for sure. Seeing little Tommy, fed and clothed, but unloved, made me take a long, hard look at myself and what I was doing to Beth and James. Wrapped in my own grief, I couldn't see straight. By moving into Josh's house, I thought that I was doing all that was necessary, fulfilling my duty, but, as you pointed out, providing the basics aren't enough—especially for kids. They need to be shown that they're loved.'

He touched her hand. 'I never for an instant stopped loving Beth and James, but if it hadn't been for you they might have thought that I had. I'd have drowned myself in work and left Kirsty and Mrs Kelly to do the important things—like giving them time and just being there.'

His bleeper buzzed. 'See you later,' he said, and strode out of the room.

One day, thought Holly, making her way back to the ward a little later, I'll give him another illustration of how true that is and tell him about young Carol and her longing to be loved as an individual.

* * *

The ward was quiet and Holly went off duty sharp at three with Jan's good wishes ringing in her ears.

'I think it's a smashing idea,' she'd said, when she'd ferreted the proposed visit to Ben's house out of Holly. 'Good for the kids, good for this Kirsty character, and most of all, good for you and Ben.'

'I thought you were against my getting too close to Ben, you said—'

'That was the old Ben. The new one is, well, different. Look at the poor bloke. He *needs* you, Holly, and that must be an entirely new sensation for him. None of his other girl friends can give him what you can.'

Holly said rather stiffly, 'You mean he needs me to prop him up.'

'Yes, in part, but then most men need propping up from time to time, they just don't admit it like women do. We're talking egos here, "Me Tarzan—you Jane."'

'Ben admitted that his ego was fragile.'

'He would, he's big enough to admit it—not many men can do that.'

Kirsty and the children flung open the door of the elegant Regency house—which reminded Holly of the Forties Club: same black railings, same scrubbed steps, same shining brass—before Ben had a chance to turn his key in the lock.

'We've been waiting for you,' bubbled Kirsty, her round girlish face, framed by thick flaxen hair, flushed and smiling. It had to be Kirsty. The full warmth of the smile, Holly noted as smoky grey eyes surveyed her intently, was directed at Ben.

Ben performed the introductions as they stepped into the spacious, high-ceilinged hall. 'Holly, this is Kirsty Larsen—Kirsty—Holly Brown.'

Tentatively they shook hands and murmured, 'How do you do?' They were both on edge.

She's suspicious, thought Holly as she turned to greet the children.

Meeting Beth and James was like meeting small replicas of Ben—or, Holly supposed, their father, Ben's twin. Both children had the same chestnut-brown hair with reddish tips; both had hazel-green eyes set wide apart beneath broad brows; but their mouths were fuller and their noses pert and slightly tilted at the tips. Perhaps like their mother Anthea?

Unselfconsciously, they offered small hands and said, 'How do you do?' when Ben introduced them.

Holly was enchanted. 'They're lovely kids,' she murmured to him as they followed the children and Kirsty down the wide hall to the kitchen.

Nursery tea in the vast, warm Regency kitchen was happy and boisterous. It was like being at home in the farmhouse kitchen, Holly thought, with her mother presiding over the teapot and her small nieces and nephews, mouths ringed with jam like Beth and James, laughing and giggling.

Squashing a wave of homesickness, she looked up and caught Ben's eye.

'All right?' he murmured.

She smiled. 'Fine,' she murmured back, and, to cover her off-guard moment, pushed James's mug of milk towards him. 'Go on, love, slurp it down,' she said.

James clapped his hand over his mouth and spluttering with laughter, turned to Kirsty. 'Holly said—*slurp*—is that a rude word?'

Kirsty shook her head and her thick blonde hair swung across her little-girl face like a curtain. 'Not exactly rude,' she said hesitantly. 'It's a sort of—'

'A slang word, a Billy Bowman word,' cut in Holly.

'A Billy Bowman word?' asked Beth in a puzzled voice, her little face puckered into a frown. 'I've never heard of a Billy Bowman word.'

'Billy,' explained Ben, 'is one of our patients, a small boy not much older than you, Beth, who comes out with all sorts of funny words.'

'Is he a very sick little boy?'

'He has been; he's getting better now.'

'What's wrong with him?' Beth persisted.

Kirsty, suddenly the figure of authority, clapped her hands above her head. 'Stop, no more questions, you'll wear Uncle Ben out, and, anyway, it's bath time. Come on, race you up the stairs.' She pushed back her chair.

James scrambled off his chair and grabbed hold of Holly's sweater sleeve. 'I want Holly to come too,' he said.

Holly glanced quickly at Kirsty. Would she mind sharing the kids' bath time with an almost stranger? Ben had been so sure that she would welcome her, but Holly had her doubts. Kirsty, she thought, had been cautious when they had been introduced. After all, she had known and loved Beth and James all their young lives. And now that their mother was dead, automatically filled her shoes.

She had every right to resent someone whom she might regard as a rival. It was a subtlety that most men wouldn't appreciate, even Ben with his uncanny sensitivity.

A rival! What the hell was she thinking about? A rival indeed, when Ben had made it plain that he was not looking to her as a substitute mother—and she certainly didn't want to be one. But Kirsty didn't know that. Perhaps if she did help with the baths, she'd have a chance to reassure her on that point.

She smiled at Kirsty. 'If I wouldn't be in the way, I'd like to help,' she said.

Kirsty gave her a long, assessing look. 'You'll get soaked,' she said.

'I don't mind, I'm used to it. I bath kids every day.'

'Then OK, just as long as you understand,' said Kirsty.

They both knew what she meant, thought Holly, and it had nothing to do with getting wet. She tacked herself on behind the children as they filed noisily out of the kitchen.

Ben, sounding rather puzzled, obviously aware of some tension, but not understanding it, said, 'I'll clear the table and stack the dishwasher and then I'll be up to read to the kids.'

Kirsty tossed her head. 'OK,' she said indifferently over her shoulder.

Holly's heart sank. She's cross with him for bringing me here, she thought, and she wants him to get the message. I wonder where he got the idea that she wanted to meet me? Either she put on a good act or he was doing a lot of wishful thinking. I'm not sure that anything I say is going to make any difference.

The children's bathroom, like the kitchen, was vast. The walls were painted in shocking pink and cream stripes and radiators against each wall were painted to match. The three tall windows were curtained in vivid poppy-red with animals rioting all over them, and the sills were crowded with rich green ferns and other evergreens. An artistic hand had been at work, thought Holly, to harmonise old and new, and clearly money had been no problem.

The Victorian rose-patterned bath on gold claw feet was vast too. Ignoring Holly, making no attempt to make polite small talk, Kirsty filled it with bubbly, steaming, scented water whilst Beth and James struggled out of their clothes.

Holly chatted to them, but kept her hands stiffly at her sides, stifling the desire to help them. The expression on Kirsty's face told her that it would be fatal to do so.

The children, seemingly unaware of the pregnant silence, sat at each end of the bath; the gold taps were in the middle. An assortment of waterproof toys bobbed about on the surface.

'Going to bomb you,' shouted James, swooping a plane down towards one of Beth's sailing boats.

'No, you're not,' shrieked Beth. 'I'm going to shoot you down.'

'Can't,' James screeched. 'Sailing boats don't have guns…I'm coming. Whee-ee.'

Undercover of this noisy exchange, Holly gathered her courage and murmured to Kirsty, 'You know, I have no intention of muscling in on your territory. Ben and I are simply friends and colleagues—we were friends before this terrible accident.' She crossed her fingers; that was stretching it a bit.

Kirsty surveyed her with cold grey eyes. 'So why has he brought you here? He's never brought any of his other girlfriends here.'

Again Holly opted for the straightforward approach. 'I'm not his girlfriend. He knows how much you are missing Anthea and thought that you might appreciate meeting a woman of your own age. He says you've been marvellous taking her place with the children, but he worries that you don't get out enough.'

Kirsty's voice was as cold as her eyes. 'I've never wanted to go out much. This is my home, this is my family. I came here when I was sixteen, just before Beth was born. Anthea was nineteen.' She put out her hands and stroked both the children's heads. 'This is where I belong, they don't need anyone else, and Mrs Kelly is my friend.'

Holly stared at her implacable face. She'd seen that look before on a young face…of course—Carol Smith. So was Kirsty another orphan needing the love and care of a family? Was that how she'd landed up with the Harveys? She must ask Ben. But right now what was she going to do or say to Kirsty, who obviously felt threatened?

She was saved from making an immediate decision by the appearance of Ben in the doorway.

'How are you doing?' he asked, adding, 'Want any help?'

'You can dry James while I do Beth,' said Kirsty, pointedly excluding Holly.

Ben looked at Holly, his face and eyes reflecting embarrassment. 'But Holly—' He broke off.

Holly smiled. 'You go ahead,' she said. 'In fact…' she made a show of looking at her watch '…I really must be going. I'm expecting a call from a friend in the wilds of Africa who sometimes has a job getting through. I'd like to get back to take it.'

It was a wafer-thin excuse. Neither Kirsty nor Ben believed it—Ben knew it to be a blatant lie; she'd said nothing about a phone call when she'd agreed to come this evening.

Ben opened his mouth and she gave him a dagger-like look, daring him to contradict her. The children were still playing noisily and still unaware of the undercurrents flowing between the adults.

Holly bent over the bath and said, 'I've got to go, kids. Thanks for letting me join in your tea party.' She stood up and blew them each a kiss and began moving towards the door.

'Why, why've you got to go?' they sang out in unison.

Keep it simple. 'Something's come up,' she said. She waved. 'See you, kids—night—don't let the bugs bite.'

Satisfied, they giggled and waved as Holly whisked out, closing the door firmly behind her, hoping that Ben would get the message and not follow.

If he did, he ignored it. It opened as she sped down the stairs.

Holly stopped. 'Go back—please, Ben, I can see myself out. I'll explain tomorrow—belicve me, it's better this way.'

CHAPTER SEVEN

BY THE following morning, Holly was wondering if it *was* the best way.

She had spent a traumatic night tossing and turning and trying to decide if she had simply taken the coward's way out by leaving Ben and the children when she had, or whether it had been the responsible thing to do. Perhaps she should have stayed and tried to convince Kirsty that her motives were purely friendly and meant to be helpful and that she was in no way a rival for Ben's or the children's affections.

Awake half the night, she overslept, had a rushed shower and, with no time even to have a cup of tea, arrived in Sister's office halfway through change over.

Sister Birdy looked up from the report as Holly slid into the room and fixed her with one of her beadiest stares. 'You couldn't have chosen a worse morning to oversleep,' she said in an expressionless voice. 'I'll finish the report, Staff Nurse Brown, then fill you in on the first half, but, believe me, your feet are not going to touch the ground for the rest of the day. We've something of a bed crisis on our hands that's got to be sorted stat.'

The crisis had arisen because there had been an accident on the main road not far from Lizzie's. A number of children, travelling with their mothers in a factory work bus to spend their day in the crèche, had been involved and injured.

Some were already in A and E being examined and assessed.

'We're not yet sure how many children we'll be asked to take,' Birdy explained. 'Dr Ben's down in A and E now helping to assess. I believe there are ten or twelve kids involved, in all. Because of the nature of the accident, it's taking a while to free some of the passengers, children included. So we don't know yet what to expect or how severe some of the injuries might be.'

She glanced round at the ring of nurses crowded into the office. 'There are a mixture of ages. Any babes of course will go to Post-natal, broken bones obviously to Orthopaedics and so on where specialist treatment is required. Which means that we may be asked to accommodate convalescing children from those wards to make room for the new admissions—plus some direct injury cases.'

'Are these in addition to our admissions already expected today, or are these going to be put on hold?' somebody asked.

'At this moment in time, I don't propose postponing anybody.' Birdy's mouth was set in the firm line that they all knew only too well. 'Some of them have waited long enough for admission—if necessary we'll shuffle around and make room. There are one or two little ones ready for discharge—Ben will sort those out when he gets back.'

Again she looked round at the ring of experienced nurses. 'It's going to be a tough day, folks. I don't have to tell you what admission and discharge days are like— lots of paperwork…' there was a concerted groan '…and with so many of them today we're going to have a lot of parents coming and going—some a help, some a hindrance, but all of them concerned and needing attention and careful handling.

'Now, plan of action—Bob, you take your gang…' she smiled at the surgical staff nurses '…and organise things on your side—I'll be over soonest to lend a hand. Jan, you and Holly take care of admissions and discharges on Med. Take young Carol Smith with you—let her see how things work under pressure. The rest of you sort out general ward work, sharing out Jan and Holly's specials between you.'

There was a general murmur of assent and eye telegraphing of messages between the nurses, all professionals used to working together.

'So…any questions—suggestions?' Birdy paused. 'No! Right, then, the sooner we get cracking, the better. I'll keep you up to date with what's happening.'

Returning to the ward, Jan and Holly found young Carol and briefed her. She was thrilled to be included in their team and couldn't wait to get cracking. Eyes shining, she asked what she could do.

'Basics first. Raid the linen room and load up a trolley with sheets, blankets, pillow slips and towels,' instructed Holly.

Carol gaped.

'And guard it with your life,' added Jan. 'Everyone is going to be on the scrounge for absolutely everything, and God knows when supplies are coming up from the laundry.'

Carol's elfin face puckered up. 'How am I supposed to guard it?'

'Use your initiative kid.' said Jan. 'Chain it to your wrist or something.' She grinned. 'It's them or us.' She nodded toward two nurses changing a bed, with an already well stocked trolley beside them.

Carol's face cleared. 'OK, I get the message, it's war,'

she said as she whisked off in the direction of the linen room.

Holly and Jan raised eyebrows at each other. 'She'll think of something,' said Holly. 'She's a resourceful kid…now, plan of campaign.'

They did a quick recce of the ward. There were three planned discharges, three planned admissions. They were easy to sort out, simply replacing the children who were being discharged with the children being admitted; it was the unknown admissions that were difficult to plan for. As yet, they didn't even know how many there would be, or what other wards they would be coming from.

'At a guesstimate shall we say a possible six?' suggested Jan.

Holly groaned. 'So, with one spare empty bed, that leaves us with five beds to find. And even if Ben decides to discharge another three of the borderline cases who *could* go home, we're still looking for two beds. Can't see how it can be done.'

'We're allowed to put up an emergency bed.'

'So we're still one short…'

'Perhaps there won't be six to be accommodated.'

There were seven to be accommodated, Ben told them when he returned from A and E.

Holly, who had spent half the night wondering how she was going to face him after her speedy, unexplained exit from his house yesterday evening, found that it was easy when there were far more serious work problems to be dealt with. Any embarrassment virtually faded away.

'So, how are we going to produce seven beds?' she said. 'We've worked out that if we discharge three borderline cases, and that's iffy until you've seen them, and put up an emergency bed, we would still be one short—

and that was when we thought we had six to accommodate. Now we're talking seven. And, of course, we still
have our three planned admissions—though bedwise they
are catered for and not due in till this afternoon.'

Ben said grimly with a trace of despair in his voice,
'Do you know something? I haven't a bloody clue at the
moment, and I've yet to figure out how to find beds across
in Surgical.'

Holly thought sadly, The old Ben wouldn't have
sounded like that, defeated before he started; he would
have been much more positive, authoritative—made a
joke of it, even. But this Ben looked so hopeless, his
shoulders hunched, his eyes dull, when only yesterday he
had at times seemed almost his old self, it was hard to
believe that it was the same man.

She felt a terrific surge of affection for him. Was he
being so negative because the accident brought his own
personal tragedy into focus? And was he doubly vulnerable because children were involved? After all, he'd just
come back from A and E—which was probably looking
like a bomb site right now, with hurt and bleeding children.

The old Ben would have hated it, but taken it in his
stride—but this Ben... She met his eyes and she knew
that he had read her thoughts. He must think she was
accusing him. She felt her cheeks reddening.

He raised an eyebrow and all but shrugged, as much as
to say—I am what I am.

But you're not, she wanted to say. 'This isn't the real
you.'

In a flat voice he said, 'A and E are dealing as fast as
poss—two of the badly injured kids will be going to IC,
others direct to Chests or wherever appropriate—it's those
wards, already overloaded, who might need to transfer

some of their convalescing youngsters to us. There will be three, maybe four, coming directly to us for observation—cuts, bruises and shock, and one of them query internal injuries.'

His lips tightened. 'But the others... No wonder they call us the bric-à-brac ward—dustbin ward, more like.' His voice was heavy with sarcasm.

Holly found herself clenching her fists. She could have hit him. He had always been proud of the fact that General Medicine could handle anything—were in the front line when the hospital was bulging at the seams; boasted that they weren't inhibited by being specialised. It was on the tip of her tongue to say, For God's sake pull yourself together, but of course that was just what one didn't say to anyone in the depressed state he was in.

Jan either hadn't noticed or was perhaps deliberately ignoring the sarcasm. 'So how many children are involved?' she asked. 'I've lost count.'

'Fourteen—apparently the bus should only have been carrying twelve with their mums.'

'It figures,' said Jan dryly. 'Some mum taking a chance and smuggling an extra kid on board who should be at school.'

Ben frowned. 'Yep, you're right, and looks like we've got one of them. Most of the kids are fives and unders. We've got an eight-year-old—he wasn't belted in. He's the query internal injuries.' He took a deep breath, straightened his shoulders, gained an inch or two. His dull eyes were suddenly alert. 'But at the end of the day, they're all kids who need taking care of. So if one of you would come with me, we'll do a round and sort out the discharges to make room for the more needy.'

The change was astonishing, he was a different man. He looked from Jan to Holly. 'Well, come on then, troops, let's get on with it.' From out of the depths he produced a quirky smile and, as if a curtain had been pulled aside, there was a glimpse of the old Ben.

Holly felt a ripple of relief trickle down her spine at the suddenly confident note in his voice. She returned his smile with a dimpling one of her own. This was more like it. For a fleeting moment back there she had thought that he was going to cave in.

'You go with Ben, Holly, and sort out the discharges,' said Jan. 'Carol—when I can find her—and I will make up beds and deal with the first admissions, then we'll get together and take it from there.'

Sister had been right about their feet not touching the ground.

Ben and Holly whizzed round the ward checking on the children who were fit enough to be discharged, or who might be sent home for a short break.

'That way,' said Ben, 'we can quickly re-admit them again when the crisis is over and before the bed manager gets her greedy little hands on the beds.' He sounded cheerful, almost bubbly. He peered over Holly's shoulder at the list she and Jan had put down as possibles, and she was acutely aware of his soap-scented cheek almost touching hers.

For the moment it was almost…almost as if the last few weeks hadn't happened. There had been no plane accident—his brother was still alive. Ben and she were just embarking on a fancy-free relationship…

Ben pointed to one of the names. 'Colin Weaver, yes, definitely he can go. He's been in for a long time, and if his parents had been more sensible about feeding him he might have gone home weeks ago. His diet's beginning to pay off now and I think he knows it—he's steadily losing weight. We'll discharge him on a strict diet regime, give his parents a good talking-to and instructions to make a weekly visit to my outpatients' clinic. He's back in if he gains as much as a kilo.'

He slanted her another smile. 'If I'm not around, it'll be up to you to put the fear of God into his mum and dad.'

'It'll be a pleasure,' said Holly as their eyes met briefly. It was wonderful to have this glimpse of the old Ben, even if it didn't last.

Another child's name caught his eye—Nicola Ford, a five-year-old who had been admitted suffering from frequent attacks of pharyngitis. She was nearing the end of a ten-day-course of penicillin.

Ben had seen her briefly the previous day. 'She's that bright little thing who chats non-stop, isn't she?' he asked.

'That's right. Smashing kid. She was admitted with a sky-high temp a week ago. But that's been stable now for three days. Her parents have been agitating to have her home. They're a sensible couple, and can obviously cope. They'd whip her back in if the need arose. I think her GP pressed for admission when her temp refused to come down.'

'Right. I'll give her a once over, but from what you've said it looks as if she's safe for discharge. I'll write to her GP, and see her in Outpatients in a week's time.'

Holly made a note on her clipboard. 'OK, that's two down and two to go. What about Lucy Parfit? Eleven, diabetic, admitted for stabilisation, has been with us for eight days. Insulin and glucose levels now stabilised. First time we've had her in as the family's just moved into the area. You were called away and missed her yesterday; you said you'd see her today.'

'Why was she admitted?'

'She was hypoglycaemic, her diet got out of line due to moving house. Up to then she'd been managing her own injections and diet brilliantly. She's another child with what seem to be sensible parents. They only lost track on account of moving and the father starting a new job. Mr King saw her on admission and saw her again three days ago at his diabetic clinic—I've got his assessment with her notes. He wants to see her again next week—she could attend that from home.'

Ben's eyes were thoughtful—he looked at Holly without seeing her.

'Well, obviously I've got to examine her and look at her past history. One's got to be so careful with young diabetics. I think I'd like her in for a bit longer to make sure all is well. And I'd like to have a word with Basil King before committing myself—he's the expert.'

He refocused his eyes until they met hers. Holly was struck by how warm and intelligent they were—like velvet. They weren't exactly merry as they had once been, but all the recent bleakness had gone. He had such expressive eyes; they changed so quickly, reflecting his moods. She wanted to reach out and touch him before they changed again… Hell, no, she didn't, she was in the middle of the ward—on duty.

She breathed in—hard.

He was saying something… 'But I take your point about her being well adjusted, and I know you and Jan wouldn't have suggested her were you not pretty sure that she could manage. Tell you what—we'll hold her in reserve if we get desperate, and I'll let her go home for a few days. Now who else do you think we might consider?'

'Well, these are outsiders—I don't think you will consider either of them for discharge but you might give them home leave for a few days. Richard O'Shea, ten, came to us from Cardiac a week ago after surgery. He's needing several weeks' convalescence which they thought he would tolerate better with us, in what they call our more relaxed atmosphere, than by remaining in Cardiac. *Relaxed!*' she repeated wryly. She pulled a face and Ben chuckled.

'Well, we are, you know,' he said, 'compared to the high-pressure stuff going on up there. And who else?'

'Nelson Franks, nine, the cystic fibrosis kid who's been a bit up and down since he picked up a chest infection a few weeks ago, but he's good at the moment. His mum and dad both know the physio drill and are only too ready to take care of him again, and they have an extended family who are willing to help out. That's all, I'm afraid. There isn't anyone else.'

'Then I'll see all of these children and make a decision, and the powers that be can stuff it if I can't come up with the beds.'

'What'll happen to the injured children if we can't take them?'

'They'll be trundled round till beds can be found for them elsewhere.'

Holly's face registered her dismay. Ben said gently, 'We'll do our best—at the end of the day it's all anyone can do.' He took her arm and squeezed it. 'Come on, let's go and look at our likely candidates.'

It was strange and comforting to have him back in the role that suited him best—that of being sure of himself and back in authority. How could she have ever doubted that he would rise to the occasion? Holly wondered as they went from bed to bed and she saw him at work, producing his own particular brand of magic as he examined and talked to the children reassuring them, making them laugh.

Looking at his calm, smiling face, she thought, Who would have guessed that he was a man shouldering a whole host of personal problems, to which her last night's action had probably added? She shoved the thought away. Time to think of that when she was off duty. Ben obviously had decided to wipe it out of his mind—at least protem.

By mid-morning they had admitted the three children directly from A and E for observation and treatment to cuts from flying glass and other debris. There was a three-year-old, Pansy Holmes, and Peter Jackson, the eight-year-old, and Fiona Cragg, four. All of them were in shock, and came up from A and E with drips *in situ* to restore their fluid balance. Although they had been given painkillers and were lightly sedated, they were tearful and wanted their mothers.

'There, love, is that more comfortable?' asked Holly, stroking back blonde curls from Pansy's bruised forehead.

Tears trickled down the little girl's cheeks. 'I want my mummy,' she sobbed.

'I know you do, sweetheart,' said Holly. 'And she'll get here to see you as soon as she can.' She crossed her fingers; she had no idea how badly injured the mother might be. 'But Daddy will be here soon.' She slipped her hand under the pillow and slightly raised Pansy's head. 'Have a sip of water, love, and then go to sleep. I bet Daddy will be here when you wake up.'

'I wish we could give them a bit more time,' she murmured to Jan, who was going through the same procedure with Fiona in the next bed, and getting much the same response.

'So do I,' agreed Jan, 'but just at the moment time's at a premium—the other kids will be coming from the other wards any time now.'

Together they settled Peter, who was the last to come up from A and E, and instructed Carol to keep a watching brief.

'I'll be back frequently to check their drips,' Holly promised Carol, 'and to take their temperatures and pulses and blood pressure, but if any of the drips stop, or you're worried about anything, let me know. Or don't hesitate to call one of the other staff nurses if you've got a problem.'

She turned away and then turned back. 'Oh, and you can give Pansy and Fiona sips of water if they're thirsty, but not to Peter. He mustn't have anything by mouth until we know that he hasn't any internal injuries, but you can moisten his lips with gauze dipped in water. Now, you're sure you'll be OK?'

'I'll be fine,' said Carol brightly, clearly relishing the trust being put in her. 'I promise to tell you at once if there are any changes.'

For Jan and Holly, coffee-break time came and went, though they sent Carol, under protest, for hers when there was a brief lull between admissions.

'It's one of the thousand rules, kid, that observer students have regular breaks, and you're already late taking yours. The powers that be don't care if the old guard—' Jan lifted her hand to include Holly '—drop dead over a bedpan, just as long as you're fed and watered. So be a poppet, no argument, take a half-hour out. We'll be glad of your input when you get back—there's a hell of a lot to do yet.'

They both watched her almost skipping out of the ward. Holly groaned. 'Were we ever that young and enthusiastic?' she said. 'Where on earth does she get the energy? I'm almost on my knees.'

Jan laughed. 'You can talk. You're not much older than she is, but what about me? I can give you—what…? Fifteen years and two teenage sons. How the hell do you think I feel?'

'Like the venerable veteran that you are.' Holly chuckled. 'By the way, I've been dying to know—where did you find Carol hiding when you went in search for her?'

'Would you believe, locked in one of the staff loos with the trolley full of linen?'

'I told you she was resourceful,' said Holly.

Holly, who was on an eight-hour shift, should have gone off at three, but didn't get off till after six when all the discharges and admissions had been dealt with. No way could she leave Jan, who was on a long day till nine, to cope on her own or with casual help.

A very reluctant Carol had been sent off at two, bitterly complaining that she wasn't in the least bit tired and could make herself useful.

'I don't doubt that you can,' agreed Jan, recalling how practical she'd been, helping with the three scared children who had come up from A and E.

She had given the two little girls sips of water and moistened Peter's lips faithfully throughout the morning, and had also kept up a good line in patter which they seemed to find reassuring. She seemed to have the knack of saying the right thing.

As the mums of all three children had been injured and taken elsewhere for treatment, her help had been invaluable whilst they'd been waiting for friends or relatives to arrive.

'You've been super this morning,' said Jan, 'but it's

those rules again. Holly and I would be for the chop if
we let you stay on any longer. But you know, love, you're
a natural—do you think paediatric nursing is for you?'

Carol looked surprised. 'What else would I do?' she
said.

What indeed? thought Holly when she finally went off
duty. If she and Jan had needed reminding why they had
ever gone into the demanding profession of nursing,
Carol's unbounded enthusiasm and tenderness with the
small patients would have given them the answer in no
uncertain terms.

And Carol had made her mark with Ben when he
whirled in late morning to examine the new admissions
and found her ministering to the children.

'Bright kid,' he commented, when Holly had sent her
off to help with dinners and she'd skipped off down the
ward. 'You must have looked just like that at her age: full
of beans, very alert and raring to go.'

'As opposed to looking old and haggard and obviously
scraping the barrel for enough energy to put one foot in
front of the other,' Holly replied tartly, but keeping her
voice low. They were standing near the foot of little
Pansy's bed—the sedation had caught up with her and she
was asleep, but it was possibly a light sleep.

Ben's eyes swept over Holly from head to toe. 'No,'
he said softly, his eyes resting on her face, 'as opposed
to looking composed, professional, yet warm and loving...at least, where your patients are concerned.'

Were the pause and the 'at least' significant? wondered
Holly. Was there a link with last night and her hasty de-
parture? Was he implying...? She stared into his eyes,
trying to find an answer. He stared back.

'I think,' he murmured, 'that I'm owed some sort of

explanation, don't you?' And before she could answer, 'Oh, not here, not now—this evening perhaps, if we can ever get away.'

So it *was* about last night, and he *was* owed an explanation.

She didn't want to hurt him, let him down, but somehow she would have to explain that the arrangement they had entered into just wasn't going to work Kirsty's attitude had made that plain. She had reached that conclusion in the small hours of the morning, and Ben would have to accept it.

Tonight wasn't a good time to talk after a long, stressful day, but it would have to do. Putting it off would make things even more difficult—and painful, for her as well as Ben.

Her heart felt as if it were being squeezed—hard. She didn't want to sever this special bond that friendship with Beth and James might have forged, but Kirsty's reaction had made it impossible to pursue.

'All right. My flat whenever you come off duty.' He opened his mouth as if to protest, but she shook her head. 'It doesn't matter if tongues wag, does it? They'll soon know that there is nothing to wag about—and as you told me on our first date your reputation's already set, and mine, well I don't care about mine.'

'That was before.' He compressed his lips for a moment. 'Before the accident. Things are different now. With Beth and James to care for, it'll never be like it was before…the roving registrar has been caged for ever.'

Holly continued to look steadily into his hazel-green eyes. 'Well, the offer's there, Ben, my flat if and when you feel like it, but no way am I going out to one of your fancy pubs or clubs. If we're going to talk, let's do it properly.'

Little Pansy stirred and whimpered in her sleep, and they both took a step nearer her bed.

Ben lifted her chart from the foot rail. 'OK,' he said, 'about nine, I should think. Now give me a run down on this infant.'

Holly glanced at the clock—nearly seven, bags of time before he would come. She would shower and change and then think about food. For once, she didn't feel hungry, although all she'd had during the long day were a few sandwiches that Sister Birdy had wangled from the cafeteria for herself and Jan and Holly.

The three of them had gobbled them down in Sister's office at some time during the afternoon, washing them down with fragrant coffee from the percolator that was one of the few luxuries that Birdy allowed herself.

'Leave a couple of sandwiches for Ben,' she had said. 'He's going to pop in for a bite if he can make it. The poor lad must be starving and whacked out. I think he must have been to half the wards in the hospital checking over the kids to come to us, and some of them are going to be arriving any minute now,' she'd said, looking at her fob watch, 'so it's back to work, ladies.'

So I'd better feed the brute, Holly decided, recalling that conversation.

Her shelf in the communal kitchen cupboard revealed a couple of tins of soup and her fridge space a cheese and pineapple pizza. Great, they could both be warmed up when he arrived, whatever time that might be.

CHAPTER EIGHT

BEN arrived at a quarter to ten. Holly took one look at his exhausted face, pushed him into a chair and put a whisky with a dash of water into his hand.

She said firmly, 'Relax, doze off if you want to, I'm going along to the kitchen to rustle you up some food.'

'You're a bossy woman,' he muttered and took a swig of whisky.

She came back with a laden tray fifteen minutes later. His eyes glazed, he was staring at his empty glass.

'That,' he said, 'was a life-saver.'

Holly plonked the laden tray down on a low table and pushed it towards him. 'Eat,' she commanded, 'and I'll pour another...you are going home by taxi, I take it?'

He nodded. She took the glass to the cupboard and filled it, and took it back to him.

He sniffed the soup with his nice, slightly craggy nose. 'Smells good.'

'It's out of a tin but it's got a splash of sherry in it. Get stuck in.'

He took a few spoonfuls. 'Aren't you eating?'

'I already have—you know me, I was starving—but I'll have a small whisky with you.'

Holly watched him in silence as he worked his way through the soup and a large wedge of pizza.

He heaved a sigh of contentment when he'd finished and stretched out his legs, and raised his arms up above his head. His face looked a little less tired in spite of his jaw being shadowed by stubble, his cheeks more rounded,

117

the lines about his mouth less marked. What a little food does for a man, thought Holly—and found herself longing to run her finger round his stubbly jaw.

'That,' he said, 'was manna from heaven.' He wiped his mouth with a paper napkin. 'You certainly know how to take care of the inner man, Staff Nurse Holly Brown,' he added.

'It's a priority on a farm,' said Holly. 'Even in these days of computers and farming by numbers, the cows still have to be brought in from the fields, no matter what the weather; sheep have to be lambed and we have our emergencies just as medicine does. It's hungry work.'

'You miss it still, don't you—the country, your family?'

'Yes, but I'm beginning to love London too, the little I've seen of it, street beggars and all.' Holly took a sip of whisky and held up her glass. 'Dutch courage,' she said, 'before you start tearing me off a strip.' We're shadow-boxing here, she thought. Putting off the moment of truth.

'Do you deserve to be torn off a strip, Holly?'

Holly met his eyes over the rim of her glass. 'For ducking out without explaining—yes, it was cowardly and rude. For the reason I did it—no.'

'What was your reason for doing it? I thought everything was going like a bomb. The children loved having you there. It's a great privilege to be invited to share their bath time.'

'Kirsty didn't share the children's enthusiasm—and I think you knew she might not, didn't you, Ben? You knew she'd got a thing about you? You should have warned me, not given me all that spiel about her needing another young woman's company. I should have appreciated your being honest about it. As it was, you dropped me right in it. She could have scratched my eyes out.'

Ben lowered his eyes and stared into his glass, then looked up at her again. 'Yes, you're right, I should have come clean, but I thought, if she met you…'

'There'd be no competition with an oldie like me?' Holly gave a wry smile. 'And she'd be willing to be friendly.'

The shocked expression was genuine. 'Hell, no, I thought she might succumb to your charm like everyone else seems to. Besides, you're only a few years older than she is.'

Holly was momentarily taken back—did she really have that much charm? Then she shook her head. 'Not a few years, Ben—she's an incredibly young twenty-two and I'm a mature twenty-six, touching twenty-seven. To her that's old, but it doesn't stop her seeing me as a threat.'

'A threat, because of me? What nonsense. I've never given her the slightest reason to think that I'm interested in her as anything but the children's nanny—friend of the family. In fact I've always lumped her in with the children.'

'And she was quite happy with that when your brother and sister-in-law were alive—being one of the family was all that she wanted. But things have changed—now she sees herself as mistress of the house, and you…well, you're the obvious master, aren't you? For her it's a simple equation. She may be immature, but she's all woman, and perhaps more dangerous because womanhood has been suddenly thrust upon her.'

'It's ridiculous, and if she thinks you're old what does that make me?'

'Oh, come on, Ben, with all your experience of women you must know that a well-heeled, good-looking bachelor in his thirties is very, very desirable. A few grey hairs—

not that you've got any—only make him more sexy and distinguished—and for Kirsty, you're everything she needs in a man. I bet she sees you as half lover, half father-figure.'

Ben shuddered. 'I don't believe it,' he said. 'I just thought she had a bit of a crush on me, triggered off by the trauma of the accident, and that it would go away. I didn't dream it might come to this—what the hell am I going to do, Holly? Where does this leave the kids? They depend on Kirsty; they depend on me—we're their family.'

Holly met his eyes. They were half puzzled, half fearful. He didn't deserve this extra problem. Again she felt that she wanted to hug him, tell him everything would be all right—but she stopped herself, though she wasn't sure why—just a simple, comforting hug.

No, wrong, wrong, wrong, hugs could turn into... She mustn't give him the wrong impression, mustn't allow that to happen.

'I don't know, Ben, but all I can say is that most problems can be solved. We'll just have to apply ourselves to it, won't we?'

'Does "we" mean you're going to help me? I thought after you'd bolted yesterday that you were through with me—almost convinced myself that it was a good thing, that it wasn't fair to involve you and I could manage on my own...but I took one look at you this morning, Holly, and knew bloody well that I couldn't manage without you—and that threw me.'

He took a deep breath. 'Suddenly everything seemed on top of me. I didn't know how I was going to get through the day. And then I saw the expression on your face and knew that I just had to. The least I could do was my best for the kids on the ward.'

'And you did,' said Holly. 'Once you rallied you were almost like your old self. You were absolutely super, coping not only with the children, but with distressed parents and relatives. You came through with all flags flying, Ben.'

'And that was down to you, Holly. I could feel you willing me on to face up to the situation.' He drained his glass and put it on the side table, and stood up. 'So you see, love, just how much I need your help. I don't see how I'm going to resolve this messy situation without it.'

Holly put down her glass and stood up too. 'Well I haven't any brilliant ideas at the moment...' she smiled up at him '...but you know what they say about two minds...'

Ben cupped her face in his warm hands and stroked his thumbs across her cheek-bones. Her spine tingled from top to bottom, the hairs at the nape of her neck felt as if they were being fanned by a cool breeze. She snatched a sharp breath.

He said softly, 'And with a mind like yours, we've got to win through in the end,' and, lowering his head, he kissed her, first on her nose and then on her mouth. It was a short, firm, unsexy kiss—a kiss to seal a friendly alliance.

Holly froze for a moment, a surge of surprise, anger and disappointment washing through her. All geared to remind him that her willingness to help shouldn't be read as anything more than a friend helping a friend, she was decimated by this cool, detached, apology of a kiss.

But why the hell do I feel like this—so shattered, betrayed? What sort of kiss was I expecting? Slowly she drew away from him. Isn't this exactly what I wanted? Didn't we agree to be friends, just friends? Wasn't I afraid that if I got involved with the children it would mess up our precious, no-commitment friendship?

There was space between them now, but their eyes were still locked together…together…the rest of his face was a hazy blur—only his green-brown eyes were there, glowing, burning into hers—there was nothing else…no sound except her drumming heartbeats. She felt the blood draining out of her face.

Ben's voice came to her from a distance.' Holly, what's wrong? My God, you're as white as a sheet.' His hands were on her arms, his fingers biting into her soft flesh, he was lowering her to the floor, and then she was blessedly flat. She closed her eyes, the room swam round her—her legs were being lifted higher and higher.

The room stopped going round—carefully she opened her eyes. Ben was peering down at her looking grim and anxious.

She raked up a weak smile. 'It's all right, Doctor, you can put my legs down now. Panic over.'

He lowered her legs slowly. 'Are you subject to fainting?' he asked, for a moment very much the doctor.

'No way, this was definitely a one-off. Anyway I didn't completely lose consciousness so it wasn't a true faint.'

'You could have fooled me.' He straightened up. 'Hell, Holly, don't scare me like that again.'

Holly began to push herself up. 'Stay put for a few minutes,' he ordered. He slipped a cushion under her head. 'I'll get you some water.' He poured mineral water from the bottle in the cupboard and knelt down beside her. Gently he lifted her head and held the glass to her lips.

She gulped the water down. 'Now can I get up?' she murmured. 'I feel such a fool lying here.'

'OK.' He helped her to her feet and steered her into the

most comfortable chair. 'Now,' he said when she was seated, 'if you're not in the habit of fainting, what triggered this one off?'

You, she almost said, but that was ridiculous—and anyway, it wasn't true, couldn't be, a modern woman in the twenty-first century, just didn't faint because her man didn't come up to scratch on the kissing front. *Her man! My man!* But he isn't. Her temporal pulse banged away. For heaven's sake, I'm not in love with him...*I'm not!*

'Whisky on an empty stomach, I guess.' There was some truth in that.

'You said you'd eaten.' He sounded accusing.

I lied, she wanted to say, but then she would have to explain that when she'd known he was coming, her appetite had simply faded away, and he'd want to know why. She invented a headache.

'Couldn't eat much. I've had a headache simmering nearly all day and a touch of nausea—not surprising considering the general racket that was going on. The ward was like Piccadilly Circus in rush hour, with kids shouting and bawling.'

Ben challenged her. 'I don't believe you,' he said flatly. 'You're used to the ward being like bedlam and the sound levels going off the scale.'

'Well, that's my explanation,' replied Holly, her voice as flat as his, 'and it's all you're going to get so you can take it or leave it.'

'What did I do, Holly? Why did you suddenly go cold on me? One minute you're your usual competent self, the next...'

Suddenly Holly felt unbearably weary. 'Leave it, Ben. We're both tired—it's been that sort of a day. We'll sort things out tomorrow—the children, Kirsty, everything.' Thank God she was on a nine o'clock start tomorrow.

His mouth twitched into a sardonic smile. '*Everything* is a bit ambitious,' he said, 'but perhaps we can have a crack at it. Now go to bed and get a good night's sleep. Thanks for feeding me and for the whisky—much appreciated.' He moved to the door and opened it. He still looked anxious. 'Good night, love, sleep well. Let's hope tomorrow is an altogether less traumatic day—on every front.'

Exhausted as she was, sleep was a long time in coming. Resolutely she refused to think about why she had fainted, but she went over and over the other events of the day, especially the incidents that involved Ben.

She recalled the despair on his face when he had come back from A and E—despair which he'd said she'd helped him overcome. Then she remembered how he had suddenly rallied, become almost his old self; a wave of pride washed over her to think that she might have been instrumental in bringing this about, and she smiled into the darkness.

It was good to feel that she had been able to help him in a practical way, so that he'd been able to deal with one problem after another with his usual caring efficiency. He was generally good at problem solving, she thought, especially other people's problems. Look at the way he had set the ball rolling for poor little Tommy Warner...

She hugged herself tight. Yes, he was good at other people's problems, at coming to their aid—not so brilliant at solving his own. For that he needed her help. But then, prior to his brother's death, he'd had few personal problems that had needed resolving—like me, she thought. We neither of us had any problems when we went out on that first date. That date seemed a long, long time ago...

*   *   *

Her mobile ringing just before seven woke her.

'How are you?' asked Ben when she put it to her ear. His voice was low and husky, quite unlike his usual clear tones.

Her heart performed extraordinary acrobatics in her chest and she suddenly found that breathing in was painful.

With an effort, she orientated herself—of course, she'd nearly fainted the night before; he was concerned about that. 'I'm fine—Ben, where are you ringing from?'

'Sister's office…and any minute now I'm going to be trampled to death by day nursing staff. It's nearly take over time.'

Her heart was beginning to settle into its correct space. 'Why are you in so early? I should have thought after yesterday's marathon you'd have made a later start this morning. After all, you are the boss man's assistant and you have got junior colleagues to share the workload with.'

'I was called in to look at young Peter Jackson, the boy with the possible internal injuries—he started passing blood in his wee a couple of hours ago, and was in a lot of pain, poor kid. We've scanned him again—it's his kidneys. One of them's pretty badly damaged so we might have to consider surgery.'

He breathed in deeply. 'Someone's coming down from the kidney unit and our revered consultant himself, the blessed Jeremy Kerr, is coming in for a conflab, so I'd better get moving and be on the doorstep to meet him. See you later, love. Glad you're feeling better. We're going to need every pair of hands again today; everywhere's still bursting at the seams.' Abruptly he replaced the receiver.

Nice to know you're needed, Holly thought wryly as

she replaced the mobile on the bedside table and sank back on the pillows to digest what Ben had told her. Personal thoughts vied with professional. He'd sounded so husky when he'd asked how she was. Husky and sexy. At least, that was how she'd read it. But perhaps she was wildly wrong about that; perhaps he was husky because he was tired and the sexiness was all in her imagination.

Considering the coolness of last night's kiss, it almost certainly was a figment of her imagination. Her reaction to him then, and this morning, shocked her. What the hell had her heart been doing, out of control, jumping all over the place?

She sat up and punched the pillow and hugged it on her knees. 'Just don't complicate matters, woman,' she said loudly. 'Stick to your original arrangement, be a good friend, be a good nurse and colleague, let that be enough.'

Be a good nurse! A vivid picture sprang to mind of little Peter Jackson lying inert much of yesterday, and now his future was in the balance. She could see Ben and the august, hook-nosed, grey-haired Jeremy Kerr, and the consultant from the kidney unit, gathered round the child's bed, deliberating about whether the badly damaged kidney should be removed or not.

Whilst the anxious father, sharing his time between visiting his wife, who had been severely injured and was in the general hospital half a mile away, would be hovering, begging for news.

It would be safe enough if the other kidney was sound—Peter would be able to manage with one kidney for the rest of his life—but if there was a query on that too?

She sprang out of bed and made for the shower. To hell with being on at nine o'clock no way could she wait till then to find out what was going on. She had specialled

Peter all day yesterday with help from Carol; she needed to know what was happening to him.

Don't let your professional life spill over into your personal affairs or vice versa, she had been warned early in her training, but this wasn't the first time she'd ignored that advice—and been glad of it.

'Come in if you're not going to waste my time,' came Sister Birdy's voice. Sharp, Holly guessed, because she was snowed under with work.

Holly slid into the office and stood just inside the door, hardly daring to breathe, waiting to be acknowledged.

Sister raised her head. 'Holly! What on earth are you doing here? You're not due in till nine. I should have thought after yesterday's marathon you would be glad of a lie in.'

It had seemed like a good idea to offer to come in early on what looked like being another busy day, but standing here in front of Sister, who was eyeing her closely, she wondered if she might appear too eager.

Honesty was the best policy. 'I heard about little Peter Jackson and wondered if you wanted someone to special him whilst waiting for a verdict from the VIPs. As I was looking after him yesterday, it seemed like a good idea…'

Birdy's rather stern face relaxed into a broad smile. 'It is a good idea. I take it the grapevine's been busy—would I be right in thinking that a certain registrar has put you in the picture?'

Holly nodded.

'Right—sensible chap, our Ben' Her nearly black eyes twinkled. 'Oh, I dare say he had other reasons for ringing you, but it wouldn't have escaped his notice that we're a bit thin on the ground this morning and another pair of hands wouldn't come amiss.'

Holly's heart plummeted. That was virtually what he'd said. So had he phoned just to establish that she was well enough to work today? Had the husky, anxious enquiry as to how she was feeling been genuine? *Of course it had*, her common sense told her. He's a good, caring friend just as he's a good, caring doctor.

And a good, caring uncle, reminded a little voice at the back of her head, who needs your help. Somehow she had to find the strength to give him that help without messing up their friendship...

'Are you all right, Holly?' Birdy was asking. 'You look a bit white round the gills. I appreciate your offer of help, but I don't want any heroics. Perhaps another hour or so in bed is what you need.'

'No, I don't, Sister. I promise you, I'm raring to go.'

Birdy gave her another shrewd, searching look, and nodded. 'OK, in that case go and relieve Pat Cunningham. She's specialling Peter at the moment. She'll bring you up to date on the obs and so on—she can start the early drugs round.'

Peter, filled with painkillers, was half asleep half awake, but recognised her from the previous day, though he had been somnolent much of the time. He was flatteringly pleased to see her. He was still on a drip infusion of fluids and not allowed anything by mouth, so, in between taking his temperature, pulse and blood pressure, Holly continued to moisten his lips with ice water and chat to him reassuringly.

About forty-five minutes after she had relieved Pat, Ben arrived at the bedside. Peter was dozing.

Ben's eyes, luminously green rather than brown, met Holly's over the small boy's sleeping figure.

'I'm glad you came on early,' he said 'I hoped you would.'

'I rather thought that's what motivated your call,' said Holly dryly.

'It wasn't you know. You're dead wrong about that. I was concerned about *you*.'

The candour in his eyes, expression on his face and in his voice told her that this was true.

She felt a fool and was aware that colour was crawling up her neck and into her cheeks. Peter stirred, his eyes flickered, he murmured something and she bent over him and swabbed his lips once more with ice.

'It's all right, love,' she said softly. 'We'll soon make you more comfortable.' She looked across at Ben. What's happening? she mouthed. What was the verdict by the VIPs?

Ben moved to the end of the bed and Holly moved to stand beside him.

'That they'll probably have to operate. Today's scan showed signs of kidney damage or disease before the accident—yesterday's scan was fuzzy. From what we've learned from the father, he's not been well for some time—that's why he was off school yesterday. He was standing up when the accident happened and got flung all over the place. Thank God there were no signs of head injury, but he was vomiting and doubled up with abdominal pain when he arrived in A and E, which seemed to indicate a stomach or intestinal injury rather than kidneys.'

Holly nodded. 'It certainly seemed the most likely diagnosis. He didn't complain of serious back or groin pain or anything else indicating kidneys and there was certainly no blood in his urine yesterday. His output was a bit scanty, but that was to be expected considering shock and dehydration. So was the first sign of kidney involvement when he started to pass blood?'

'He began to complain of back pain around about mid-night. The new houseman, Mike Todd, was on duty. He increased the analgesic, but it didn't work, and a couple of hours later the haematuria started. That was when I was called in.'

So he'd been up since about two o'clock—and he hadn't left her place till eleven, and yet he'd still bothered to ring and find out how she was feeling. Well, right now, thought Holly, I feel mean as hell for doubting him earlier.

His enquiry had been genuine even if he had almost pushed her into coming on early after he'd established that she was OK. Fair enough, he was entitled to after being up half the night himself and knowing they were stretched staffwise. Again the overwhelming desire to give him a hug surged through her. But she kept her arms stiffly at her sides, and said huskily, trying to inject her feelings into her voice, 'Ben, you're a marvel. Not many registrars of your rank and experience would have turned out in the night as you did—they would have left it to one of their underlings.'

To her surprise, he went faintly pink beneath the light tan which had persisted into the spring after a winter ski-ing holiday.

'That, I take as a compliment coming from a hard working, dedicated nurse like you, Holly.' His voice was gruff. 'Whatever—I felt that this little lad needed all the help he could get—and since I was here yesterday…' he shrugged '…it seemed the right thing to do. Peter's parents don't seem to have appreciated how unwell he's been for weeks, or they would have taken him to his GP. As it is, I suppose, one might say it was almost a lucky ac-cident—it might have been weeks, months, even, before kidney damage was diagnosed—might even have been too late.'

'And now?'

'He'll be going up to the kidney unit soon, and they'll do their best to sort him out. There's a good chance they can save one kidney. I want you to go up with him, Holly, and see him settled in the nephritic ward, as his dad's not around and we haven't been able to get in touch with him. Poor bloke's cutting himself in two trying to see both his son and his wife.'

'Thanks. I'd like to go with Peter and stay with him for a bit. I'm sure it'll be OK with Sister Birdy, and I dare say Sister on Kidneys will be glad of someone to keep an eye on him.'

'She'll be only too pleased, her ward's on regular take-in today.' Ben moved closer and put a hand on her bare forearm and she could see the tired bruising beneath his eyes. 'And, Holly, talking of getting sorted out, I want us to get sorted out too… Like you said last night, two minds are better than one—do you think we might meet up for lunch, say one-ish?'

His touch was light, but a tremor ran up her arm like an electric shock. She ignored it. 'If the gods are with us and don't throw any more emergencies in the way, I'll try to get off for one o'clock.' She kept her voice cool, rather distant, though she felt as if she'd won the lottery at the thought of lunching with him. Her breathing was ragged, and every pulse in her body seemed to be working over-time to keep up with her thumping heartbeat.

Oh grow up, she told herself in disgust as Ben strode away and she turned back to Peter.

Ben was seated just inside the door to the cafeteria with a laden tray on the table when Holly arrived just after one.

What on earth was he sitting there for where the world

and his wife would be passing? Any sort of conversation would be hopeless—why hadn't he chosen a table on the far side near the windows?

She opened her mouth to ask when he forestalled her, stopped her in her tracks by his beaming smile.

'I have here,' he said, waving at the tray, 'a princely offering of salad and chicken sandwiches, apple pie and custard and tea—the so-called coffee being undrinkable. Does that meet with your approval.' And, not waiting for her answer, 'I thought we might take it up to your room where we'll get some sort of privacy.'

He sounded bubbly, on top of the world.

The cool nerve of the man! *Déjà vu!* He'd not only chosen her food, which was exactly what she fancied, but this time had gone even further and practically commandeered her flat. For a moment Holly was speechless, and then said the first thing that came into her head.

'So you're not worried any more about your precious image—the one-time roving registrar is ready to come to my flat in broad daylight...' Her voice trailed away. It was the cheapest of jibes—he'd explained why his former image was an embarrassment to him with his new commitments.

Mean! If only she didn't feel so nervous, so gauche, wasn't so skin crawlingly aware of him. To have a cosy chat with him in her room, where only last night...

The smile was wiped from his face, which suddenly went very still, and his eyes, warm and friendly a moment before, turned to stone.

She was appalled. 'I don't know why I said that.' The words stumbled out of her mouth. She sat down in the chair opposite him with a bump.

'Neither do I.' His voice was without expression. He looked down at the table and rearranged the cutlery on

the tray, then abruptly raised his head. His eyes were neither stony nor friendly, but sad. 'What have I done, Holly?
Why do you keep blowing hot and cold? Are we friends,
or are we not?'

What did he mean, *she* blew hot and cold? How dared
he? That was what he'd done ever since his brother's accident. The urge to contradict him surged through her, and
then died away as suddenly as it had arisen. He had a
good enough reason, she had none—at least none that she
could tell him about. That was a secret that she must keep
to herself.

Holly looked straight at him, keeping her eyes glued
on his. 'Oh, Ben, of course we're friends,' she said softly,
'and all I want to do is help. Let's go up to my flat, and
talk…' She grinned. 'Oh, and eat, I'm…'

His eyes brightened, burned into hers, the tension fell
away. 'Starving,' he suggested.

They had less than half an hour to talk and eat by the
time they'd traversed the ground-floor corridors and
reached her flat, but suddenly, with the air cleared between them, they immediately got down to dealing with
the Kirsty problem.

Ben swallowed a mouthful of sandwich. 'I did a lot of
thinking in the small hours, once I had done what I could
for Peter. Clearly my first duty is to Beth and James. They
need Kirsty, so I will have to tread warily, *but*, I mustn't
allow her to rule us all, which is what she has been doing
for the last few weeks. I must take the blame for that,
because I've depended on her too much—I guess that's
what's given her the idea that I'm attracted to her. I made
a point of letting her know how grateful I was for all that
she was doing—I suppose I overdid it.'

Holly nodded. 'Understandable, but tricky striking the right balance. So how do you intend to put things right?'

'For starters, tell her that I haven't any romantic feelings for her. I'll do it as gently as I can.'

'Well, that's obvious, but if it doesn't work? I've a gut feeling that she'll fight to the last…if you'd seen her the other night when the children were having their bath. She means business, Ben. You're what she needs to make her world complete and she's not going to pass that up lightly.'

'Yes, I realise that I must take that into consideration.'

'And?'

His mouth quirked up at one side. 'I shall have to make it plain that I'm already spoken for, produce a fiancée— it's the perfect solution, and would allow Kirsty to back off without losing face.'

Holly paused with a sandwich halfway to her mouth. He couldn't mean…wouldn't expect… *He could—he would.* There was no mistaking the meaning in the luminous hazel eyes that met hers across the table.

He clasped her hands, which were still holding the sandwich, between his. 'It would only be for a short while, Holly, and we would know that it wasn't for real—we would soon be able to return to just being friends, and by then Kirsty would have got over her crush, or whatever it is she has for me, and things would return to normal.'

His beeper beeped insistently. He dropped her hands. 'May I?' He gestured to her phone.

Holly nodded, her mind numb.

Ben's voice filtered through. 'I'm on my way.' He strode to the door. 'Think about it, Holly, please. It's neat, it would solve everything with the minimum of hurt to everyone.'

CHAPTER NINE

FOR an unknown length of time, Holly sat staring at the door through which Ben had disappeared. His last few words buzzed round and round in her head till she felt it might explode.

'It's neat, it would solve everything with the minimum of hurt to everyone.'

The minimum of hurt! It would hurt me like hell, she wanted to scream.

She covered her ears with her hands to shut out the words, but they were still there like a fly buzzing against a window-pane. Every other sound and thought was blotted out.

After a while, feeling like an old woman, she dragged herself to her feet and made for the bathroom. She stared at herself in the mirror over the basin. Blue eyes, usually sapphire-bright, stared back at her dully, her normally sleek cap of tawny hair stood on end. She almost smiled. 'I look like Billy Bowman' she mouthed to her image in the mirror.

She was sloshing her face with ice-cold water when her mobile sprang into life, breaking through the buzz in her head. Water dripping down her chin, she wandered, zombie like, back into the sitting room and picked it up.

'Yes?'

'Is that you, Holly? Are you all right? You sound weird.'

'I'm fine…is that Jan?'

'Of course it's Jan. You'd better get your skates on,

you're long overdue from lunch. Sister's at a meeting or she'd have your guts for garters.'

Holly heard herself giggle and had to struggle to stop. I'm hysterical, she thought. 'You do use some funny old-fashioned expressions, Jan…'

'I know, I sound like your mum; that's because I almost could be.'

'Actually,' Holly said, enunciating very carefully—for some reason, her lips, like the rest of her, felt numb, 'you sound more like my granny.'

'Thanks a bunch, you've made my day,' Jan said dryly and then added anxiously. 'Holly, are you sure you're all right? You don't sound like yourself at all.'

Holly took a deep breath. 'Jan, stop worrying. Like I said, I'm fine, I'm the same old me.' It wasn't true, but it sounded good and would keep Jan from probing too deep.

She went through the rest of the day on automatic, resolutely shutting out her extraordinary lunch-time conversation with Ben; if she thought about it, she'd explode or burst into tears. She avoided Ben too, whenever she saw him on the ward, dodging into the furthest bays and once into the staff loo.

They were busy, but not as busy as the previous afternoon. Little Pansy Holmes and Fiona Cragg had recovered sufficiently from shock and their minor cuts and bruises, and were discharged home. But the two empty beds were filled as soon as they could be remade with clean linen.

A four-year-old boy, Henry Potter, suffering from acute gastroenteritis, was admitted into Pansy's bed. He was severely dehydrated and arrived from A and E, hooked up to an intravenous drip of normal saline and glucose to replace fluids lost through diarrhea and vomiting.

Sister directed Holly to special him and the other child

expected in that afternoon. Since Ben would be in any minute to examine the small boy, this meant an end to her avoidance tactics.

'OK, Holly Brown, keep it cool and professional,' she told herself, mentally squaring her shoulders.

She was holding a kidney dish under Henry's chin with one hand and supporting his hunched back as he retched painfully into it with the other when Ben appeared.

'How's it going?' he asked softly as he slid between the curtains. He unhooked the temperature and fluid balance chart from the bed rail.

At the sound of his voice, Holly felt colour creeping up her throat and kept her gaze firmly fixed on Henry. She nodded at the receiver. 'As you see, very little coming up so his stomach's pretty well empty; but this constant retching is exhausting the poor little chap. Do you think we can start pushing fluids by mouth. He's on max flow by drip.'

Henry finished trying to vomit and leaned back, eyes closed, against the pillows piled against the head rest. This, Holly had discovered within a few minutes of his arrival, was the position he found most comfortable. It relieved the abdominal pain better than when he was lying flat.

Ben moved to the side of the bed and picked up the child's drip-free hand. Very gently he pinched the skin on the back of the thin hand. Henry frowned and opened his eyes.

'It's just a little test, Henry,' explained Ben, as the skin slowly—too slowly—smoothed out. 'It tells me how much your body is getting dried out because you've been sick such a lot, on account of this bad tummy ache. That's why you've got this tube in your hand—it's dripping in special water, and now we're going to start giving you special water by mouth, just a sip at a time.'

Henry shook his head vigorously, his mouth trembled. 'Can't drink, it makes me more sick.'

'Not the way Nurse Holly gives it,' said Ben. 'That's right, isn't it, Nurse?'

Henry was looking from one to the other. Holly had no option but to look at Ben.

He was smiling. Mindful of Henry's scrutiny, Holly smiled back, and then transferred a wider smile down to her small patient.

She bent low over the bed and whispered in his ear. 'If Dr Ben agrees, I can magic my water pink and because it's pink it goes down easier—and it'll also help to take your tummy ache away.'

Henry looked thoughtful for a moment, and then lifted his head. 'Can I have some of Nurse Holly's pink water?' he asked Ben.

Ben made a great thing of studying Henry's chart. 'Do I take it, Nurse Holly,' he said *sotto voce*, laughter in his voice, 'that the magic ingredient is some of Sister Birdy's famous pink vegetable colouring?'

Holly nodded, then, bracing herself to speak to him, said flatly, 'That way we can encourage him to swallow some pink paracetamol for the pain and kill two birds with one stone.'

If Ben noticed the flatness of her voice, he gave no sign of it.

He lightly cuffed the small boy's shoulder. 'I think some of Nurse Holly's pink magic water is definitely on,' he said, 'and you should get stuck in as soon as possible, just a little drop at a time. When you've had a whole mugful, we'll be able to take this—' he pointed to the cannula connected to the drip tube '—out of your hand, because you'll be feeling much better by then, less sick, and your body will be fast making up for the fluids it has lost.'

The small white face looked almost animated. 'I bet I get through a mugful in, in…'

'Two flicks of a lamb's tail,' suggested Holly. 'That's what we say on the farm where I live.' Holly crossed her fingers behind her back; only her granny said that, and then rarely.

Henry's eyes rounded. 'Have you got lots of lambs on your farm?'

'Hundreds—now, while Dr Ben's here I'm going off to get your pink medicine and your pink water, and when I come back I'll tell you about the farm.'

Ben was waiting for her outside the cubicle when she returned carrying a tray bearing a plastic jug, mug and a bottle of paracetamol and a spoon. He wasn't smiling, but he didn't look angry, just rather thoughtful.

'Henry's parents are with him,' he said. 'I've written him up for paracetamol and Maxolon, five ml four hourly, PRN, and fluids by mouth, ten ml at a time, to be gradually increased. Go and get him started, I'll wait for you here.'

Holly made herself look him straight in the eye. 'On a personal level we have nothing to say to each other, Doctor.' And before he could reply she whisked into the cubicle.

She stayed there as long as she could, but once she had started Henry off on a sip of water—he gagged, but kept it down, and followed it up with the paracetamol and the anti-nausea syrup, Maxolon, followed by another sip of water—there was no reason for her to stay with him. His parents were sensible and only too pleased to have something to do by feeding him the water.

'Press the buzzer if you need me,' she told the Potters. 'I'll be back in a quarter of an hour to check his temperature and pulse.'

Reluctantly she slipped out between the curtains and looked cautiously up and down the ward. Good, no sign of Ben. If she could make it to the nurses' station...

'Going somewhere?' His voice was silky and close to her ear.

'Where did you spring from?' Holly hissed, stepping to one side and putting space between them. Even so, the unusual aftershave, soap, whatever it was that he used, triggered off a reminder of the morning they had met, weeks ago—or was it a lifetime ago? Life had been so different then, the future clear, bright, uncomplicated.

'From the next-door cubicle.'

'You were eavesdropping,' she accused.

'That's right,' he said blandly. 'Wanted to make sure you didn't take avoiding action—again.'

So he had noticed her diving and ducking in and out of cubicles.

Holly inhaled a deep breath, expanding her lungs and diaphragm. Her heart pounded uncomfortably in her chest. 'What does it take, Ben Harvey, to convince you that I have nothing to say to you on the personal front?'

'There's nothing you can say, except to explain yourself.' He took a step and filled the space that she had created. He laid a hand on her arm. 'What's wrong, Holly? If you don't tell me, how the hell can I put it right?' He sounded sad and frustrated, his eyes were gentle.

Holly felt her hurt and fury building up. 'If you need telling, Doctor, there's not a hope of putting it right.'

Ben stared into her blazing blue eyes—she *was* beautiful when she was angry, but nothing in the world would have made him use that corny old phrase. He leaned forward and planted a kiss on her mouth. 'Then I'll go away and think about it,' he murmured. 'I'm rather good at solving conundrums.' He no longer sounded sad—in fact he sounded almost jubilant, as if he had made progress.

'And smug with it,' said Holly through clenched teeth, and, sidestepping him, stalked off down the ward, her back, she hoped, making a statement for her.

She stayed in the staff loo for nearly ten minutes pulling herself together; rearranging her features; waiting for the crimson in her cheeks to subside and her heart to return to its rightful place.

Sister Birdy was standing a few yards down the corridor in the doorway of her office when Holly came out of the loo, talking to some anxious parents. 'Hang on a minute, please, Staff Nurse,' she said as Holly drew level. 'I'd like a word. Mr and Mrs Michell are just leaving.' She shook hands with the departing couple and turned back into her office.

Holly followed her.

'Sit down,' she commanded, and sat herself down behind her desk. She shuffled some papers around and then looked up. 'You look bothered, Holly—care to tell me about it?'

'Not really, Sister, it's a personal matter.'

'Well, you know my rules on that, don't you? You either leave your problems behind you when you enter the ward, or you put me in the picture.'

'Yes, Sister, I'm sorry. It won't happen again.'

Birdy put her hands prayer-like beneath her chin and looked thoughtful. She swung her swivel chair from side to side, and then nodded. 'Holly, you're a good nurse, my sort of nurse, the children's sort of nurse, and I want to keep you on my team. That means being at your best. I think you need a few days off to get yourself sorted. You've got days off tomorrow and the next day. I suggest you take two more days off in lieu of overtime—you've worked a fair bit already and can make up the rest when you get back—unless you're desperate for the cash.'

Holly shook her head. 'I'm not bothered about that, but will the office people wear it?'

'They'll love it, my dear—anything that means that they don't have to write a cheque thrills them to bits. All they require is a chit from me saying that you're entitled to the overtime, and I'll do that right now.' She pulled a pad towards her and scribbled furiously. 'There we go, attach that to your time sheet and hand it in at the end of the month.'

She swivelled round to examine the duty roster on the wall behind her. 'You'll be due back on Tuesday. I'll put you down for a three to ten, that'll give you the morning free—should you have trains or something to catch.'

She'd got to be a witch or a prophet, thought Holly, to know that I wanted, needed to go home, breathe some good Shropshire air. She put down her mobile after an hour of phone calls and being shunted from one office to another. But, finally, her seat was booked on a train the following morning, changing at Birmingham, which would take her to Shrewsbury, the nearest station to home, and a return seat on Tuesday at eight, a through to Euston, which would get her back in time for duty.

Four clear days at home. Well, almost four, excluding her travelling time tomorrow, and she could use that time to think—or perhaps sleep; that had been in short supply recently. And by this time tomorrow she would be helping Mum stack the dishes in the dishwasher...and she and Mum would have talked...

She showered, and took that thought to bed with her. But her last conscious thought as she drifted into sleep was of young, vivacious Carol Smith, who now had a mum she could talk to.

But though her last thought was of Carol, she dreamed about Ben. All she could remember in the morning was that the dream seemed to go on all night in fragmented parts, little scenes, and each scene seemed to end in the same fashion: Ben was walking towards her through a golden morning mist, holding Beth's hand on one side and James's on another, and they were all smiling.

Her mobile rang as she was about to leave the flat. She knew it was Ben. Should she answer it?

'Yes,' she said, her voice brittle.

'I think I've got the answer to the conundrum.'

'Good.'

'Don't you want to hear it?'

She steeled herself. 'Not now, I've got a taxi waiting—goodbye.'

She switched off and let herself out of the flat and spent the journey trying to forget the sound of his voice and calm her bounding pulse.

'Dad.' Holly flung herself against her father's broad chest and felt his muscular arms wrap round her in a bear-hug. He was in good shape for sixty. 'What a treat. I thought one of the boys would come to fetch me because you would be too busy with the end-of-month accounts.'

Her father grinned. 'What, stuck in behind a computer on a brilliant morning? No fear, I pulled rank and left Roger wrestling with the April balance sheets.'

Holly pulled a tragic face. 'So it wasn't because your

youngest daughter was coming home you deigned to meet me, but just to get out of doing the books?'

'Something like that.' Paul laughed and, to show what he really felt, gave her another hug. 'Come on, let's get a move on or your mother will have kittens.'

They reached the farm forty minutes later, the Range Rover eating up the miles as they bowled through the twisting up and down country lanes. They drove with the windows wide open.

Holly inhaled one deep breath after another. 'It's wonderful after London,' she said.

'There's nothing like Shropshire air,' replied her father smugly.

'Don't condem us until you've sampled our London park,' Holly could hear Ben saying on that first evening.

She defended London, or was it Ben? 'They do have *some* wide open spaces: Hampstead Heath, Regent's Park—that's near the hospital.'

'Parks!' scoffed her father as they drew up in front of the farmhouse.

Her mother was standing in the doorway. She opened her arms wide and pelted across the golden gravel of the drive as they stopped.

'Mum!' They gave each other hug for hug and kiss for kiss.

I hope I look like her when I'm crashing sixty, thought Holly, standing back to admire the still young face, the almost as bright as her own blue eyes and short, stylishly cut hair. The local hairdresser was a natural and charged half what the Shrewsbury salons did and a quarter of London prices. Hairwise, there was nothing dowdy about the women of Abbeyfield and certainly not about her mother.

Vicky Brown took the same moment to examine her

daughter's face. Noted the pain in her eyes, the set of her mouth, the jut of her chin. 'We'll talk later,' she murmured, giving her another hug, 'when your father and the others have gone back to work after lunch.'

Roger came striding out from the farm office, looking a younger image of his father, though with his mother's blue eyes and no grey in his hair. There were more hugs.

'Don't go back to the office,' said Vicky. 'We'll have lunch as soon as Holly has tidied up.'

Roger grinned at Holly as she started up the stairs. 'She doesn't change, does she? Surprised she didn't remind you to wash your hands.'

Holly grinned back. 'I wouldn't mind if she did, it's great to be home.'

Great to be mothered, she thought.

Lunch was a movable feast to accommodate emergencies or any other variable that might turn up. The long table was laid up in the kitchen; everyone served themselves.

Wendy, Roger's wife, mother of two sturdy boys, five and six years old, and looking in danger of being blown over by a decent gust of wind, but in reality as tough as they came and managing the equally tough herd of sheep like a veteran, came whizzing into the kitchen after the others had started eating.

'Holls, good to see you.' She smacked a kiss on Holly's cheek and then went over to the Aga and helped herself to soup and then sat down next to Holly. 'Sorry I'm late, Vicky, two lots of twins decided to put in their late appearance in unison.'

'They OK?' asked Paul.

'Fine, just what we wanted.'

That means ewes, thought Holly, looking round at the

pleased faces ringing the table. Any minute now we're going to be talking market prices…

Twins, even though Wendy was talking baby lambs and she was thinking of Ben and Josh, a long table and a warm kitchen, conjured up another kitchen and other smiling faces…

She closed her eyes for a moment, a beef sandwich halfway to her mouth. Perhaps she should have told Ben that she was going home for a few days; perhaps she shouldn't have put the phone down on him this morning. Conversation flowed round her. She opened her eyes and met her mother's across the table.

Vicky smiled. Holly smiled back. Her mother would understand, however much or little she told her.

Jonathan came in. He dropped a kiss on top of her head. 'Hi, little sister, how's the great big city treating you?'

'Not so much of the little sister, you're only a couple of years older than me.'

'But infinitely wiser.'

At twenty-nine, he was nearest her in age, and, as much as she had a favourite amongst her brothers, he was her favourite.

Holly snorted. 'How's Amy?'

'As ever.'

'Will I see anything of this long-suffering girlfriend of yours whilst I'm home? She is by way of being my best friend, you know, though I didn't do her any favours introducing her to you.'

'She won't hear a word against me…' Jonathan laughed '…and Mum's invited her for Sunday together with the rest of the tribe so you'll see her then for a girlie get-together.'

'Not so much of the tribe,' said Vicky. 'It's family, so of course Amy's included.'

*   *   *

Half an hour later, Vicky and Holly were climbing the footpath up the rounded hill toward the ruins of the abbey after which the village of Abbeyfield was named. Holly was puffing a bit—there weren't many hills in London. Vicky was striding along with hardly a quickening breath—she was a great walker.

She gave Holly a sideways grin. 'I think I'm in better shape than you are, love, though you've lost a few pounds and I've gained some.'

'You're telling me,' gasped Holly, throwing herself down on the short springy turf when they reached the top.

Vicky sat with her knees drawn up and her hands linked round them, looking out over the village and the farm. Holly knew that she was waiting for her to start talking.

She rolled over onto her side and supported herself on one elbow facing Vicky.

'Mum, did you have any doubts about falling in love with Dad?'

'Good God, yes, dozens, yes, especially about marrying him—I wanted to be a career woman, beginning to be possible without being a complete freak in those days. I fancied having the odd affair on the side, but definitely nothing permanent.'

'So what changed your mind?'

'Your father did. I thought he'd gone along with the idea of a casual affair, and then one day he dropped his bombshell—marriage or else…'

'Or else what?'

'He'd look elsewhere. He was right, a farmer needed a wife in those days nearly forty years ago, just as vicars did, and doctors—they needed unpaid secretaries.'

Holly shuddered. 'It's gross.'

Vicky nodded. 'Yes, it is—was. I dare say it still happens sometimes.'

'So why did you go along with it? Why didn't you stick to being a career girl and have…?'

'Sex on the side?' Vicky finished the sentence, guessing that Holly was a little embarrassed at asking her mother such a direct question. 'Because I was in love with him.' Her mouth quirked into a smile. 'Still am. He threw down the gauntlet and jerked me into realising that I'd loved him all along, and if he wanted marriage, then so did I. Oh, I knew that being a wife and mother would never be enough for me, I would have to find some way to be *me*…'

'And you have with your writing.'

'Yep—I have the best of both worlds.' Vicky stretched out a hand and stroked Holly's cheek. 'Does that help?' she asked.

'Would Dad have looked elsewhere if you'd said no?' she countered.

Vicky shook her head. 'No, he was as much in love with me as I with him, but he wouldn't actually say so. Fluffed all around it. Like a lot of men, couldn't actually bring himself to declare his love. They will use all sorts of expressions, excuses, to cover up the fact that they are in love, even invent situations not to tie themselves up, until they have to—want to. Mind you, it can work both ways—we do that too, if we don't want to commit ourselves. Doesn't matter, as long as one doesn't leave it too late.'

She stood up, a not very tall, slightly plump, smiling woman, with twinkling blue eyes and a stunning modern haircut, wearing shabby trousers and a quilted anorak.

Holly stood up too and kissed her on the cheek. 'Thanks Mum, that's all I wanted to know. Ben will love you.' In a flash it was all blindingly clear: Ben was in love with her just as she was with him. All that rubbish about pretending to be engaged. It was a smokescreen—he was protesting too much—he wanted it to be true, she wanted it to be true—what the hell were they waiting for…?

'Ben…nice sturdy sort of name. Tell me about him.'

'Well…' Holly took a deep breath and related the events of the last couple of months, from her first date with Ben to his phone call that morning just as she'd been leaving. She finished as they reached the bottom of the hill.

Vicky smiled at her as they climbed the style into the lane. 'Well, you've got a few hurdles to go, love, but if I were you I'd not let any grass grow under your feet—go for him. It's obvious that's what he wants you to do, however he wraps it up. Go along with this pretend engagement.'

'And Kirsty?'

'Work at making friends with her, she needs security. Make sure she knows that you value her as much as Ben's sister-in-law did. She'll come round in time, perhaps sooner than you think. Life's like that—throws up the unexpected in your face.'

A wind had blown up and clouds had ominously materialised in the bright sky. Vicky shivered. 'Come on, love, let's get home and have a nice cup of tea—laced with a drop of whisky, I think—and plan what we'll give the hungry hordes for supper.'

CHAPTER TEN

'WELCOME back love.' A kiss was dropped on her cheek, her weekend bag taken out of her hand.

Holly couldn't believe her eyes or her ears. 'What the hell? How the hell...?' Her cheeks blushed and paled, her heart felt as if it were about to leap out of her breast.

'Your sojourn at home hasn't improved your vocabulary,' said Ben, a lopsided grin belonging to the old Ben making her insides churn.

He strode up the platform and she had to run to keep up with him. 'I've got a taxi waiting.'

She was too breathless to argue, question him further until settled in the taxi.

Fuming with anger—or was it elation?—she turned to him. 'How did you know that I would be arriving at Euston at this time? In fact, how did you know that I had gone home?'

A smile twitched at the corners of his wide, tender mouth, his hazel-green eyes glittered. 'Sister Birdy and I put our heads together and decided that it was your most likely bolt hole.'

'I thought better of Sister Birdy than to discuss me with you.'

'She's almost as fond of you as I am,' Ben said. He took hold of her hands lying limply on her lap, and raised them to his lips. 'Though perhaps *almost* is an exaggeration. No one could feel about you as I do, not by a million miles.'

Her heartbeat tripled.

They arrived at Lizzie's. He paid off the taxi and steered her into the spacious reception area. He paused outside the cafeteria. 'Wait here, I've ordered sandwiches,' he explained. 'For you to take up and eat whilst you're changing.' He picked up a package at the counter, and put it into her hands. 'I've got to get back to the ward, there's a bit of pressure on—food poisoning at a small local private school.'

He thrust her holdall at her. 'Well, go on, scoot, it's gone half-past two.'

'But…'

He was hurrying away from her. He waved a hand over his shoulder without turning round.

By five o'clock, Holly and Jan had done three gastric lavages—stomach washouts to clear out the poison, they had explained to Carol—and cleaned up and bed-changed several other small, frightened patients.

Carol as always had been sensible and sympathetic with the children, reassuring them, gentling them along with a firmness beyond her years. 'But I didn't half feel queasy,' she admitted, 'when the gastric lavages were being done. Those tubes going down into their stomachs, and all that fluid being poured in and then being drained out again—no wonder they bawled.'

'One of those cases where one has to be cruel to be kind,' said Jan. 'I hate doing them, but if you catch them in time it clears the muck out of their stomachs before it can get round the rest of the body. You do the same for any case of poisoning if it's severe enough, and thank God it nearly always works.'

She looked at her fob watch. 'And now, kiddo, it's time you were off.' Carol made protesting sounds. 'Yep, I know it's your last day, but rules are still rules, so scoot.

With luck we'll see you again as a fully fledged student nurse. Good luck with your exams, love. Let us know how you get on.' She kissed her on both cheeks.

Holly put her arms round her and gave her a hug—Carol's face was wet. 'Come and see us any time. Here's my mobile number—don't leave it too long before you get in touch.'

Carol dragged herself up the ward and Ben passed her in the doorway. He stopped and gave her a hug and a kiss. More old-style Ben, thought Holly, and her heart pumped overtime again. Just as coming to meet her from the train without warning was old-style Ben. Yet he hadn't put in an appearance this afternoon, and even under pressure of work she had been preparing herself for another face to face.

'Oh, so the white knight has come to the rescue at last,' teased Jan.

He shared a smile between both of them. 'Sorry about that, ladies, had a bit of an emergency in Surgical, a straightforward appendicectomy that went wrong. Poor little kid had to go back to theatre for irrigation and drainage.'

'Would that be little Jonny Wheatley?' asked Jan, who'd been on the surgical side the week before.

'That's the lad, but he's doing OK now. Now, about this little lot.' He waved round to indicate the food-poisoned children, who, by much shuffling round, had been accommodated in six-bedded and two-bedded adjacent bays. 'The lab has identified the infection as salmonella, as we suspected it was. Fortunately most of the children aren't too badly affected as they hadn't eaten much of the chicken dish which caused the infection—too yucky was the general consensus. Most of them will be able to go home later tonight, or tomorrow morning.'

'That's great.' Holly's eyes met his and was amazed at the…*love?*…she saw in them. Confused and breathless, she looked down at her watch. 'I've some obs to do,' she muttered, and disappeared into the nearest cubicle.

Ben followed her. He had a few words with the small girl in the bed and with her mother who was sitting beside her, whilst Holly took her obs with shaky hands and tried to control her breathing and blot his presence out of her mind.

He took the chart from her and read the latest findings. 'Tracy's doing fine, she can go home in an hour's time,' he told her delighted mother. 'But give her plenty to drink and keep her warm and quiet for a day or two. If you're worried about her, bring her back in. Take care of yourself, Tracy.' He touched the child's cheek in the special caressing way that he had. 'Goodbye, love.' He shook hands with Mrs Bond, and ushered himself and Holly out of the cubicle.

They stood in the middle of the bay, away from the five other beds where relatives were absorbed in keeping vigil beside subdued children. He turned Holly to face him, gripped both her arms. His eyes greener, more brilliant than she'd ever seen them, devoured her. The nearness, the warmth, the almondy scent of him, washed over her, wave upon wave.

Desperately she looked round the bay. Surely someone would call 'Nurse.' No one did.

Ben's fingers pressed harder on her arms. He leaned forward so that his face was almost touching hers.

'The visitors.' Her voice was a breathy whisper.

'Think we're talking life-saving shop…'

'As we should be.'

'Nothing critical at the moment.' Their eyes melded, his fingers bit into her. 'The conundrum,' he said, his

voice as breathy as hers. 'You don't want a sham engagement, you want a real one.'

'No,' Still breathy but emphatic.

'Why not? You're in love with me!'

'*No,*' Sharp, brittle.

'I'm in love with you, Holly, absolutely, want to marry
you. Nothing to do with two orphaned kids or my
brother's death—I fell in love with you that first evening.
Went along with all that rubbish about friendship to please
you—knew it was a lot of nonsense—hoped to wear you
down in time, only events overtook us; left me a jibbering
idiot. Still would be if it weren't for you.'

'No, I don't believe it.' This time it was a whisper.
'You're not really in love with me, it's, it's—gratitude.'
Holly shook her head and Ben's bleeper beeped.

He flicked it off. 'This is a genuine proposal, think
about it,' he said, and, dropping his hands from her arms,
marched off toward the nurses' station.

Holly stared after him for a moment, then stared un-
seeingly at the clipboard she was holding. The world had
gone crazy. She had been proposed to in the middle of
the ward. On the train journey back from Shropshire she
had imagined a dozen scenarios, but not this.

'*Nurse!*'

Back to the real world. Ten p.m., the end of her shift,
seemed a long way off.

Ben was waiting for her when she stepped out of the lift
on the ground floor. She'd known in her bones that he
would be. Her tiredness fled, her heart did strange things,
but she kept her voice steady.

'I'm going to get something hot to eat,' she told him.

'I've asked them to keep back two hefty portions of

shepherd's pie,' he replied, steering her towards the cafeteria.

How did he always know what she needed? 'What, no pudding?'

'Gladys's bread and butter pudding—thought we needed an injection of carbohydrate.'

'Won't argue with that.'

The cafeteria was almost empty. Holly spread tomato ketchup liberally over her shepherds pie and took a forkful. 'Mmm, heavenly,' she murmured, her mouth full, her eyes closed.

She opened her eyes as Gladys appeared with a pot of tea, milk jug, sugar basin and mugs which she plonked down on the table. She sniffed. 'Don't say I don't ever do anything for you,' she said, nodding at Ben. 'Ain't my job to wait at table.'

Ben grinned and patted her hand. 'You'll go straight to heaven to that great big shiny cafeteria in the sky,' he said.

'What? And have my bunions giving me gyp for ever— not bloody likely.' She walked back towards the counter, and said over her shoulder, 'Give a shout when you're ready for your pudding.'

'You're a gem.' Ben winked.

Holly watched him pour out the tea, his competent hands, nicely manicured as always, rock steady.

She said softly, 'You're almost back to normal, aren't you, Ben?'

Equally softly, he said, 'Not all the way back, I hope— please God the last month or so has taught me something. How to fall in love, for instance, and how many kinds of loving there are—the subtleties of it are amazing.' His lip curled. 'I used to think I was so clever, enjoying myself, yet steering clear of commitment. Tried to be honest, not hurt anybody—but...'

'If you were as frank with them as you were with me, they had no reason to expect commitment.'

'Didn't stop some of them hoping. I feel badly about that. Didn't realise how deeply they might be hurt.' He piled their two empty plates together, and stood up. 'Better save Gladys's bunions,' he said, and strode off toward the counter.

For a moment she tried to shut down her thoughts. It had been a hell of a busy day, a weird day: a candid statement of love, a proposal—it was enough to turn a girl's head. She giggled, sipped her tea and gazed round the nearly empty cafeteria. It always had this curious atmosphere at night, with a skeleton staff on duty. It would get busier later when night staff started to come down to eat.

Ben was chatting to Gladys, making her laugh, the way he made the children laugh. She recalled Jan saying before she'd had that first date with him that he was an antidote to a grey winter's day. It was a gift, a talent, one that he had almost lost for a while. But he'd recovered it, together with an added *something*—a solidity, maturity that added to his masculine presence.

Her toes curled in her sensible duty shoes as she watched him returning to the table carrying pudding plates. She couldn't believe that in the space of a few weeks any man could have that effect on her. Especially now, when her career was really beginning to take off.

Sister Birdy had hinted at the possibility of a permanent senior staff nurse's post coming up in a few months' time, when General Medicine expanded, and her being in the running for it. An exciting prospect, and from there a short step to a junior sister's post—but now…

'There.' Ben placed a plateful of steaming bread and butter pudding, rich with sultanas, in front of her. 'Get stuck into that, love, and then to bed.' He dropped a kiss on top of her head. 'Perchance to dream of me.'

She did dream of him and again Beth and James figured in the dream, but this time Kirsty was with them. All four of them were coming towards her, the children skipping, Kirsty and Ben linked arm in arm. As they drew level, Kirsty waved her left hand ostentatiously; a huge diamond glittered on her ring finger.

Drenched in sweat, Holly woke to a brilliant May morning. She didn't remember the dream, only that it was something unpleasant. She looked out of her window down onto the courtyard dividing the staff quarters from the hospital. It was half in shadow, half in sunlight.

With all her heart she wished she were still at home in Shropshire on top of the small rounded hill that overlooked the village, talking to her mother in the shade of the abbey ruins.

What would she have to say about yesterday's events? Would she think that Ben's proposal was genuine? Or would she think the way he had made it, the place he had made it, too weird, too whimsical to be true? After all, Holly had at first. But, no, her mother wouldn't think that, for, though in many ways she was a practical, down-to-earth person, she knew much about the weird and wonderful; she wrote fantasy books for children.

Holly thought, on a wave of pleasure, I think she and Ben are two of a kind. I think they'll like each other on sight. I think she'll be pleased as Punch if I marry him.

And suddenly she had no doubts. Her mind was made up. Everything fell into place. Enticing thoughts of a nursing career going onwards and upwards went out of the window, though she'd carry on for a little while. She would marry Ben. Have kids by him, lots of kids. Provide him with the family he'd missed out on and help him look after Beth and James so that they were one big happy family...

Kirsty!

The dream flooded back in detail.

Her heart dropped to her boots.

Poor Kirsty, who fancied herself in love with Ben. The stumbling block between herself and Ben smoothly moving into a life together. On one short visit she had achieved a rapport with the children that she could build on, but just the opposite with Kirsty. Suppose Kirsty really was in love with Ben, but it simply hadn't surfaced till the accident? Maybe it wasn't just a crush as Ben seemed to think, but something that must be taken seriously.

Showering and dressing, Holly wondered if Ben had tackled the pretty young nanny, as he'd said he would. Before she could formally accept his proposal of marriage—though, in view of the style of his proposal, formally was not perhaps the word—she must know if it had already been resolved in her absence.

Not that anything would stop her marrying Ben, now that she was certain that her love for him was reciprocated. Again she glowed and warmth spread through her; she couldn't wait to get on duty and see him. Last night seemed a lifetime ago.

They met up mid-morning to snatch a coffee—and a kiss—in the staff room.

Ben pulled her to him. 'Love you,' he breathed against her willing mouth.

'Love you, too,' Holly murmured. Damn! She hadn't meant to say that—not yet. She had things to ask him and they needed more time; the children definitely needed more time to accept her in spite of the good start they'd made; and as for Kirsty…

'When shall we get married?'

Holly struggled to free herself and managed to put an inch or two between them. She tilted her head back so that she could look up at him. 'In the fullness of time,' she said, through a slightly nervous chuckle. 'I've always wanted to say that, it sounds rather grand.'

He smiled down at her, his eyes full of love and laughter. 'I especially love you when you are like this, bubbly and chuckly—so when do we get married?'

'When we've given the kids time to get used to me, accept me as a substitute mum—when Kirsty gives us her blessing, or something like it. Have you spoken to her yet?'

His arms would have pulled her closer again, but she held back. He took her hands in his. 'Yes, love, I did talk to her, I explained that you and I were engaged…'

'But we weren't,' burst out Holly, trying to tug her hands from his. 'We still aren't.'

Ben's eyes danced. 'But we're going to be, my darling, aren't we? Any moment now we'll…'

'Any moment now—what?' asked Jan from the doorway. Her eyes dropped to their joined hands. She grinned. 'That looks encouraging—am I interrupting something?'

Ben raised his eyebrows. 'Now the woman asks!'

Holly snorted. 'Jan, you're the limit, any other decent-minded person would have made themselves scarce.'

Jan's grin broadened. 'You know me.' She shrugged.

'Shall we tell her?' Ben squeezed Holly's hands.

'I can't wait, but it'll have to be after you've answered an outside call,' said Jan. 'It's a Mrs Kelly on the ward phone.'

Ben dropped Holly's hands and made for the door. 'It's got to be the kids,' he said over his shoulder, taking off up the corridor at a run.

Holly and Jan hurried after him.

'Who's Mrs Kelly?' panted Jan.

'Ben's cook-housekeeper.'

'It's not the children,' he said, when he came off the phone minutes later. 'It's Kirsty. She was involved in an accident on her way back from taking them to school. She's been taken to St Hilda's so I'll beetle over there right away. Any problems, have a word with Ken or Mike, they're both around somewhere, and let Birdy know that I'll be missing, probably for the rest of the day.'

Uncharacteristically, he fumbled shrugging himself into his jacket that he'd left draped round the back of a chair behind the station. Holly eased it up over his shoulders. 'I'm sorry about Kirsty, but so pleased that the children are OK. If there is anything I can do to help,' she said softly.

Regardless of Jan's and several other pairs of interested eyes, he kissed her. 'Me, too,' he said. 'You're off at five—come over and help Mrs Kelly take care of the kids. I'll probably be visiting the hospital—the poor girl hasn't anyone else.'

She nodded. 'Will do,' and, as regardless as he had been of the audience and several lewd comments, kissed him on the cheek.

'So you're serious,' said Jan, as she and Holly, armed with a linen-loaded trolley, started a round of the eight beds containing the food-poisoned victims.

'Deadly,' replied Holly—no use trying for discretion now, and she didn't particularly want to. Discovering that she was in love, and loved, she wanted to shout it from the roof-tops. Besides, the next few days—weeks, maybe, if Kirsty was badly injured—she wanted to be *there* for Ben, and it would be easier if she didn't have to resort to subterfuge.

'I'm glad.' Jan loaded plastic bowls onto the bottom shelf of the trolley. 'You're two nice people, you deserve each other, and the sooner you get together, the better. Now, we'd better get cracking. Let's start with our two new ones. Poor little devils, they do look rotten.'

There were still eight patients suffering from salmonella, for, although two of them had been discharged, two more had taken their place.

Giles Strachan aged six and Leila Porter, seven.

They had suddenly deteriorated, having been looked after at home. They were on strict bedrest and intravenous fluids and anti-nausea medication, as were the other acutely ill children. All these children were weak and feverish and needed skilled hands on nursing care, even to carry out simple tasks like bed bathing.

It was a job for well-trained, experienced nurses, and Jan and Holly were kept busy till after one, when they went to a late lunch.

The afternoon passed in a flash. Ben phoned Holly at four to say that he was staying at the hospital. 'Kirsty's still unconscious, but beginning to rouse. I want to be here when she comes to. Mrs K is expecting you. She's staying the night to take care of Beth and James, but will be glad of your company this evening.'

*   *   *

Will she? Holly wondered, standing on the white, scrubbed stone steps leading to the gleaming black en-amelled front door near Regent's Park, just before six. She rang the bell.

Mrs Kelly was all that a children's story-book cook should be. She was short and dumpy, with a round smiling face, rosy cheeks and thick grey hair wound into an elab-orate knot at the back of her head. Her intelligent eyes were nearly as black as Sister Birdy's.

She stood in the open doorway with Beth and James on either side. It flashed through Holly's mind that all that was missing were floury arms and a big wrap-around apron.

The two Ben look-alikes bounced up and down, both talking together...

'Kirsty's hurt, she's had an accident, Uncle Ben's with her.' Beth took a trembling breath.

'She's all bloody, I 'spect,' said James, 'but Uncle Ben will make her all better.'

Mrs Kelly's eyes met Holly's. They were warm but sad, though she remained smiling. 'Now, Jamie—Beth, where are your manners? That's no way to welcome Miss Brown. Let her get into the house first.' She had a soft voice overlaid with an Irish accent.

The children pulled her into the hall and toward the kitchen, still chattering excitedly. Mrs Kelly puffed along behind.

'They've been so looking forward to seeing you again, miss, and I've been looking forward to meeting you, though in better circumstances.' There was none of the hostility that Kirsty had exhibited.

'And I've been looking forward to meeting you, Mrs Kelly. Ben has told me so much about you,' replied Holly as the children pushed her onto a chair at the kitchen table. 'And, please, do call me Holly.'

Over the children's babbling, Mrs Kelly said, 'Oh, I couldn't do that, miss, you being Mr Ben's fiancée and one day mistress of the house. I don't believe in this new-fangled way of everyone being called by their Christian names—not right. But I'll call you Miss Holly, that's proper enough.'

Holly's heart missed several beats and her stomach churned. *One day mistress of this elegant house!* How did Mrs Kelly know of their engagement? Of course, Kirsty must have told her, confided in the old housekeeper when Ben had broken the news of their then fictitious engagement to her. She tried to suppress a wave of excitement—fictitious then, true now. She had been engaged for a whole afternoon.

Beth and James were tugging at her again, insisting that she helped them have their bath. She glanced at Mrs Kelly, still not too sure what was expected of her. The last thing she wanted to do was step on anyone's toes.

The old housekeeper looked at the clock. 'Just the right time, Miss Holly. If you get them bathed, I'll have a bit of supper waiting for them when you come down.'

The phone rang as Holly and the noisy children came back down to the kitchen. Mrs Kelly answered it and turned to Holly.

'It's for you,' she said softly, glancing at the children. 'Dr Ben. Why don't you take it in the study? Second on the left down the hall.'

Holly's pulses raced. What sort of news would she have to break to the children? They adored Kirsty. Please God, let it be good. They'd had enough heartache to last a lifetime.

'Good news,' said Ben. 'She's regained consciousness

and recognised me. She's been sedated now and will probably sleep all night. I'll be home after I've had a word with the consultant. Give the kids a hug and a kiss from me.'

By the time Ben came home, the children had been read to, reassured that Kirsty was out of danger, and were safely tucked up in bed.

'Let's go and have a look at them,' Ben said, taking Holly by the hand, after giving her and Mrs Kelly the latest news of Kirsty. 'I want to give them a goodnight kiss. I couldn't get them out of my mind when I was sitting by Kirsty's bed—supposing it had happened on the way *to* school, and they…'

'But it didn't, and they're fine, look…'

He stood between the two beds looking down at the flushed faces of his niece and nephew with a look of such tenderness on his own face that Holly wanted to cry. He dropped a kiss on each smooth forehead, straightened up and took Holly in his arms.

'When we are married,' he murmured into the soft curve of her throat, 'and have children of our own, we must make sure these two feel part of the family.'

'Goes without saying,' Holly murmured back, rubbing her smooth cheek against his stubbly one. 'They *are* part of the family—in fact, they are at the very core of the family. Look at them, they are Harveys through and through—I just hope all the little Harveys look like that.'

'*I don't,*' Ben said fiercely. ' I want a bunch of chuckly plump little girls, with merry blue eyes and crisp tawny hair, like their mother.' He snuffled the top of her head.

'Hey, not so much of the plump,' she said.

His hands slipped up under her loose sweater and

cupped her soft breasts supported by a scrap of lace. 'I like plump,' he murmured, and covered her mouth with his in a long, lingering kiss, full of promise of things to come.

CHAPTER ELEVEN

For Holly and Ben, the next few balmy May days flew past in a haze of mutual tingling pleasure and delight in each other's company. When they were near each other, they positively crackled with awareness, both at work and at the Harvey house near Regent's Park. A touch of a hand, the brush of an arm, turned Holly into a jelly without substance, and sent her blood pressure rocketing to new heights.

She spent most of her off-duty time at the Harvey house, increasing her rapport with Beth and James, and with Mrs Kelly who had obligingly agreed to live in whilst Kirsty remained in hospital.

Kirsty was making slow but steady progress; her head wound, fractured ribs, tibia and ankle were mending. Her lower leg and ankle were pinned and being brought into alignment by metal screws. It would be weeks before the leg would weight bear, but she was already receiving physiotherapy so that her muscles didn't deteriorate.

On Saturday afternoon, Ben took the children to see her. James was disappointed at the lack of blood, but thrilled with the metal pins holding together her tibia and ankle. 'Kirsty's got *nails* sticking in her leg, and she's got big black rings round her eyes, like my panda,' he told Holly when she arrived that evening, his own eyes like saucers.

She had been on a seven to six and had come straight from the hospital without changing out of uniform.

It was the first time Beth had seen her in uniform. 'I

166

like yours better than the ones the nurses wear at Kirsty's hospital,' she said, patting the epaulette on the shoulder of Holly's tunic. 'What's this for?'

'To tell everyone that Holly is a clever nurse and has passed lots of exams,' interjected Ben.

'I want to be a nurse at your hospital,' said Beth.

Holly gave her a hug. 'Perhaps you will be one day,' she said. 'But not because of our smart uniform, but because we are the best children's hospital in the world.'

When Beth and James had gone to bed and Mrs Kelly had retired for the night, Ben took her in his arms and sank down on to the large squashy leather Chesterfield.

He spent some minutes showering her with kisses and nibbling her ears, and then said, 'Kirsty wants you to go and see her. Will you do that?'

'You didn't put any pressure on her, did you?'

'None whatsoever, it was all her own idea, though perhaps sparked off by Mrs Kelly who went to see her yesterday. Mrs K is very fond of her and probably knew of her fantasizing about marrying me, and was well aware that it just wasn't on. I think perhaps she was able to persuade Kirsty that getting hitched to an oldy like me wasn't a good idea.'

Holly took a deep breath. Visiting Kirsty wasn't something she relished. 'I'm on another long day tomorrow to make up for last weekend, so I'll go on Monday.'

'Do you want me to go with you?'

'No, I think this is going to be woman talk.'

Holly took fruit and sweet-smelling early sweet peas in trembling hands and arrived sharp at two on Monday. This is crunch time, she thought. Please God let me say the right thing; it's so important to the children. Let me make

Kirsty see that her role in the household will be the same, that she is still part of the family.

Kirsty's bruised black eyes, that James had so eloquently described, were now a muddied khaki, but her injured leg was still studded with pins holding the fractured bones together.

Holly laid her gifts on the bedside locker and, the nurse in her coming to the fore, she leaned over the bed to look more closely at the damaged leg.

'I bet that's painful,' she said. 'Are they giving you something for it?'

Kirsty nodded, winced and put a hand to her head. 'And my head hurts too, but not constantly as it did up to yesterday.'

'You're on the mend,' assured Holly. 'It's amazing how quickly the body heals, especially when someone is as fit as you are, though you'll have to go easy on your leg for quite a while.'

Kirsty smiled. 'That's what Leo says.'

Has she gone a bit pink, wondered Holly, or is it my fancy? 'Who's Leo?'

'The physiotherapist, he comes to see to my leg twice a day—the good one too so that the muscles don't get weak, because it'll have to do a lot of weight-bearing when I start walking again.'

Holly stayed for half an hour. They talked a lot about physiotherapy and the progress she hoped to make, and Leo's name came up often. 'Even when I go home, I shall have to come back twice a week for physio,' she said. 'But once I'm home I'll be able to help you or Ben with the children, though bathing will be beyond me for a while.'

Holly bit back an exclamation. Had she heard what she thought she'd heard?

'And I'll be able to help Mrs K with vegetables and things, and do the ironing. I won't be able to stand for long but there's a high stool in the kitchen that I can sit on…'

Brightly she chatted on. Holly only half listened. All the careful things she had been going to say flew out of her head. They were redundant.

'There was no point in mentioning anything about being wanted and being part of the family,' Holly told Ben that evening. 'She seemed to know that it would be so. I don't know what Mrs K said to her but it certainly worked— she doesn't seem to resent me in the least, even congratulated me on our engagement.'

'Talking of engagements,' murmured Ben, 'that reminds me.' He stretched out his legs and lifted his hips in order to reach into his trouser pocket.

They were sitting side by side on the Chesterfield in front of the roomy fireplace, filled, not with a log fire on this mild May evening, but an urn full of blue delphiniums and pink lupins, picked in the large garden—well, large for London—at the rear of the house. It had been a lovely surprise for Holly.

Ben tugged a small box out of his pocket. 'We have been engaged for days and you haven't got a ring. This was left to me, together with some other jewellery, specifically for my future wife, by my late godmother. It was her engagement ring. She didn't have children of her own. I didn't ever think that I would have a use for this or the other stuff, but there you go, you walked into my life and turned it upside down.' He kissed her—a quick, casual kiss.

He opened the leather box to reveal an antique ring of delicate filigree silver, forming a cluster of lover's knots, and at the centre of each knot a glowing blue stone.

He took the ring out and held it in the open palm of his hand. 'Lapis lazuli to match your eyes, not the traditional diamond,' Ben said softly, 'but that can be remedied if you prefer a diamond or some other precious stone.'

'A girl's best friend—no, thanks—*this*—this is just perfect…' She held up her left hand and he slipped the ring on her marriage finger. Holly gazed at the glowing band. 'Oh, Ben, it's lovely, it fits perfectly, and it's twice as precious because it has a history and comes from your godmother.'

'I thought it would fit. Funny, the thing I most remember about her is her hands—they were small and competent like yours.' He picked her hands up and brushed his lips across her knuckles. 'I wish you could stay the night, love, I want you in my bed.' The green in his eyes darkened, he pulled her onto his lap and his fingers unbuttoned her blouse and slid between her lacy bra and silky flesh.

Her nipples peaked. She kissed him passionately. She murmured breathlessly, 'I'd like to stay too, love, but no way with dear old Mrs K in the house. You'll just have to contain your soul in patience.'

His chest heaving, Ben leaned his head back against the Chesterfield and studied her through half-closed eyes. 'Not my soul I need to contain,' he muttered. 'You'd better fix on our wedding day, stat, or we'll have to hire a hotel bedroom for a few hours like they do in movies so that we can make illicit love.'

'Only sleazy movies, and I don't think I could do that.'

'Not even for me?'

'Not even for you, love. I don't want anything sleazy to taint our love, it's so special. Of course there's always my flat if you're desperate, but I know that doesn't appeal. Do you think you could hang on till the middle of July?'

Ben groaned and squeezed her hard. 'That's weeks away.'

'It's my parents' wedding anniversary, they'd be thrilled if we made it a double, and, anyway, it'll take that long to arrange everything. Making sure the children understand the situation, holiday leave, booking the church…'

'I thought a register office.'

'Please, I'd like the village church where I was christened. I go to services when I'm home, it's all part of family and village life—unless you have strong reasons for not wanting it.'

'No, I don't have strong feelings one way or the other—if that's what you want.' He clapped his hand to his forehead. 'My God, I've just realised, I've yet to gird my loins and meet your parents, though heaven knows when we are going to fit that in.'

'I told you eight weeks would be barely enough,' said Holly smugly.

He met them a few days later when the Browns came up to London.

'I've managed to drag him away from the farm, but we can only stay over one night,' Vicky explained, 'but it seemed a good way to meet you and the children.'

'If the mountain won't come to Mohammed…' Paul Brown tailed off.

'Not a question of won't, sir, it's getting time off together. There's always some sort of crisis in a hospital, at present it's a summer bug laying the kids low.'

'Understood,' Holly's father said with a smile as they shook hands, 'and it's Paul. Medicine and farming have a lot in common—time is always at a premium and there's always some crisis brewing—but I had to come and give my future son-in-law the once over.'

The brief visit was a total success; everyone jelled with everyone else. For the first time in their short lives, the children had someone they could call Grandma and Grandpa.

Vicky and Holly made guest lists and plans, whilst Paul, Ben and the children kicked a ball about in the garden. Vicky undertook to speak to the vicar about the church, arrange the catering—they would have the reception at home; there was bags of room for a marquee— 'And Charlie Randall, the baker, can make the wedding cake. He's a beautiful icer.'

Holly had an idea. 'No, don't ask him yet, let's sound out Mrs Kelly. She's a wizard cook and I want her to be part of this.'

Mrs Kelly was thrilled to bits. 'Haven't made a wedding cake in years, but don't worry, Miss Holly, I haven't lost my touch. You just let me know how many we're catering for.'

'Bridesmaids,' said Vicky that evening, when they were drinking coffee and the men were watching a rugby match. 'It's all or none: your little Beth and your three nieces, or none of them, but if you plump for that there'll be an awful lot of disappointed little girls around—and what about Amy? She's been your best friend since school.'

Holly took a deep breath. She could picture Beth's dear little face lighting up at the thought of being a bridesmaid, it would further cement their already close rapport. 'Then I suppose it had better be all,' she said. 'Amy as chief bridesmaid and Jan as my matron of honour, so that'll make six in all.' She grinned a wicked grin. 'And to think Ben wanted a register office wedding.'

'Men,' snorted Vicky, and she and Holly giggled. Vicky went on to say. 'There's a boutique just opened in Shrewsbury advertising complete wedding outfits—you can hire or buy. Would you trust me to discuss what you need, for the little ones anyway? You can tie up the details on the phone.'

Holly flung her arms round her parent's neck. 'Oh, Mum, I'd trust you with my life. You sort out the girls, and I'll talk to Amy about her dress. I think it should match Jan's. Perhaps she could come up for a couple of days and we can go foraging for their dresses and mine.'

Every day was crammed full.

At work, every empty bed filled up with children coming in with 'summer flu' which was the only diagnosis that anyone could come up with. Kids came in with high temperatures, aching limbs and sometimes chest pains. Occasionally they were sick, but not always. Blood tests revealed nothing significant. It simply remained a mystery illness, and the children seemed to recover as abruptly as they went down with the bug.

'Just let's hope the media doesn't get hold of it,' Ben said grimly, when he and Holly were doing a round. 'Can you imagine the headlines? "Mystery killer virus hits children."'

'But it hasn't killed anyone,' Holly pointed out.

'That wouldn't stop them,' said Ben, pulling her into an empty cubicle and kissing her eyes, nose, mouth and neck. 'We're both off this afternoon,' he mumbled, as he nibbled an ear, 'and Mrs K is going to visit Kirsty before picking the kids up from school—the house will be empty.'

They made love in the big, canopied bed that seemed to take up half the space in Ben's large room; at first gently,

wonderingly, then passionately, explosively, with Ben
kissing every hidden place in Holly's naked, quivering
body.

He came up for air, and Holly kissed his face, glistening
with sweat. 'My turn,' she murmured, and trailed her lips
and tongue down his strong throat, lingering on his
Adam's apple and the hollow beneath it before following
the arrow of bronzed hair down to his umbilicus and beyond.

Roused to the point of no return, he grunted and pulled
her roughly up the length of his body, rolled her over and
looked down at her. 'You're a wanton woman, Holly
Brown,' he breathed heavily, and then gently eased into
her, his body heavy and welcome.

As often as they could during those summer days, they
took Beth and James out on explorations, as Ben called
them, and daily he became once more the fun-loving uncle
whom they adored. In front of her eyes, Holly watched
the old Ben and the new merge into a mature—to her—
almost perfect man, a wonderful guardian, a caring doctor
and a superb lover.

And the children responded like flowers opening to the
rain, for, although there were occasions when one or both
children became withdrawn or tearful and wanted their
mummy and daddy, these occasions were growing less
frequent, and with Kirsty in hospital they turned naturally
to Holly for comfort.

The park was a favourite expedition—to the zoo and
the boating lake, where Ben showed off his rowing skills,
skimming past slower boats, to Beth and James's
screeches of delight. Holly looked on feeling like a be-
nevolent aunt in charge of three noisy children.

Another favourite expedition was to a nearby bookshop with a large children's section, and a toyshop next door, bursting with the latest up-market toys and games—a sort of children's Harrods, thought Holly. Ben was as excited as the children, testing out train sets, tanks, heavy lorries, anything that moved.

One afternoon, they were allowed to choose something special at both shops to celebrate the engagement. 'Provided,' said Holly, who was feeling herself gradually into the mother role, 'you find some things in your toybox to give to the hospital for the sick children.'

Ben gave her a quick, warm kiss. 'You're a natural mum,' he said.

'I've had a good role model,' she murmured back.

To Ben's surprise, Beth chose a Lego set. 'I thought you would choose a doll!' he exclaimed.

'I've lots of dolls,' replied Beth. 'I want to build something.'

Predictably James chose a large expensive Scalextric set. Holly raised her eyebrows. 'He'll never manage it on his own,' she said.

Ben's eyes twinkled. 'Who said he'll be on his own?' he said.

In the bookshop, Beth chose a fantasy book written and illustrated by—Vicky Pope. 'My mother's pseudonym,' whispered Holly, 'but don't tell her till she's read it.'

'My lips are sealed.' Ben chuckled. 'Talented lady, your mum, like her daughter.'

James chose a pop-up book about farm animals.

'That'll be useful,' said Holly, 'when he goes to the farm before the wedding.'

Fetched by Roger, Holly's eldest brother, Kirsty and the children were to go up with Holly three days before the wedding, to meet the family and get to know the other children, and for Beth to try on her bridesmaid's dress.

Amy spent a couple of days in London. She and Jan meshed with each other immediately. Holly and Jan took a day off, and the three of them together went shopping for their dresses.

The mother of one of the children on the ward owned a bridal shop. 'Come and see me,' she invited, 'and I'll let you have something at cost. It's the least I can do after all you've done for Maggie.'

The bridal shop was in fact a small up-market boutique, and the prices reflected it. Holly, wondering if she could afford even a cost-price wedding dress, watched several being modelled until she saw exactly what she wanted. It was a simple Regency-style gown, creamy coloured chiffon dotted with tiny pale blue daisies, with an off the shoulder neckline and minuscule puff sleeves, and a blue ribbon catching up the soft material just beneath the bosom.

'All Jane Austen and *Pride and Prejudice*,' murmured Jan, 'and you've already got your Mr Darcy, so what are you waiting for?'

Even before she tried it on, Holly knew it was for her. 'I'll take it,' she said when Jan and Amy raved over it, 'whatever the price.'

To her surprise it wasn't as dear as she thought it might be. 'We have a good mark up,' said Mrs Jordan, 'but don't tell anybody.'

There was a dainty coronet and satin slippers and long mittens to compliment the dress.

Keeping to the Regency theme, Jan and Amy chose blue gowns with wisps of chiffon tucked into the low neckline. 'In my case to hide the wrinkles that neither of you have yet acquired,' Jan joked.

Holly rang her mother that night and described the dresses.

'Perfect,' said Vicky. 'The little ones' dresses will blend in like a dream. I've done some sketches, they're in the post, It's called the confetti collection—each dress is a different pastel shade with multi-coloured hearts scattered over them, and there are tights and shoes to match.' The pleasantly warm days of May gave way to the blue and gold days of June. Kirsty came home from hospital and cheerfully hopped around the house and made herself useful. She entered enthusiastically into the wedding preparations and brought Leo's name into the conversation whenever possible.

'Don't worry, he's got an invitation,' teased Holly. 'We couldn't let you go all the way to Shropshire without your physio.'

It had been a relief to learn that Leo was in his early twenties and single. 'I have high hopes,' Holly told Ben.

'Do I detect a touch of matchmaking?' He laughed.

'Too right,' replied Holly. 'I'm not risking Kirsty turning her eyes on you again.'

Ben looked smug. 'Jealous,' he whispered, nibbling the lobe of her ear, telegraphing a message straight to her calf muscles and turning them to jelly, so that for a moment she had to lean into him for support.

'Yes,' she said simply, and whisked herself out of the cubicle in which he had trapped her.

Replies to invitations began to pour in—as many of the invitations were for hospital staff, they expected quite a few refusals since not everyone could be off at the same time and they had to make their way to Shropshire. But, amazingly, most of them were accepted.

'I detect Sister Birdy's hand in this,' Holly said.

'The general has marshalled her forces, organised cover and rented a minibus for the day,' said Jan. 'And, working with her, the old man himself, our Mr Jeremy Kerr, has sorted out the medical side.'

Holly choked over her coffee. 'I can't imagine the august Jeremy in a minibus,' she chortled.

'Oh, he hasn't gone that far. He and Mrs Kerr will be driving up in their Roller, as befits our distinguished consultant.'

Another unexpected acceptance was from Tony Wadebridge, from somewhere deep in the heart of South America, where he was working with the Red Cross. He and Ben had been at school together and Ben wanted him as best man, but held out little hope that he would be able to make it.

'I'll be with you two days before you tie the knot,' he told Ben on a crackly telephone line. 'I can't wait to meet the clever lady who has dragged you out of your bachelor existence.'

'You can look, but not touch,' said Ben.

'Jealous?' purred Holly, who had been sitting with her head glued to Ben's whilst he took the call.

'Cautious,' he replied. 'I think it would have been wiser to leave him in the jungle... Come here.'

Holly purred some more, and snuggled up even closer on the squashy, sexy Chesterfield. 'I love it when you're masterful,' she murmured, rubbing her cheek to his.

'For all of five minutes,' he said dryly. 'Then I would be firmly put in my place by the sexiest women's libber on the planet.'

Holly gave him a smacking kiss and pulled away. 'That's enough smooching,' she announced. 'We've stacks to do yet, we've got to decide on presents for the bridesmaids, and do thank you letters for the wedding presents already rolling in.'

The days rolled by too, and suddenly it was July, a hot, thundery July and days only away from the wedding.

Beth and James were getting increasingly excited, looking forward to staying on the farm. If they settled, they were to stay there whilst Holly and Ben were away on their honeymoon. Beth, too, was itching to see her bridesmaid's dress.

At work, beds continued to empty and fill. There were a number of kids in with heat rashes and sunburn and allied reactions to the sultry weather. Billy Bowman was back in after being away for much of June—awaiting assessment for another operation.

'I hope he doesn't have it till we get back from our honeymoon,' said Ben.

'Me, too,' confirmed Holly, watching the small, bright lad with the giant charisma tear up and down the ward, re-acquainting himself with old patients and introducing himself to new. 'I want to be here to look after him.'

On Holly's last afternoon on duty, he wheeled up beside them as she and Ben left a cubicle where they had been examining a new admission. He handed them an enormous envelope. 'It's a card,' he said, 'signed by all the mums and dads and the kids.' He fumbled in the back of the wheelchair and pulled out a slightly battered plant. 'And there's this too,' he added. 'It's a g'ranium. Mum says you can plant it in the garden. It's red,' he further added unnecessarily.

Holly blinked back tears and Ben cleared his throat. 'It'll be perfect in a tub on the terrace,' she said, and dropped a kiss on the scrubbing-brush head.

CHAPTER TWELVE

FIVE o'clock on her wedding morning! Holly leant on her window sill and looked out over the swells and dips and hills of the Shropshire countryside, as she had since she was a small child. And in the distance, regal and alone but a familiar friend, shrouded in early morning mist, The Wrekin, the most famous of Shropshire hills.

She breathed in great hungry lungfuls of air, just as she had on her visit months ago. Then she had come home to sort out her muddled feelings about Ben. And she had— and today they were to be married. She smiled and took in another deep breath. It was already warm, but tasted of dew and brambles and ferns. Petrol fumes and hot, humid London were a million miles away.

The sun was rising over Abbey Hill in a sky streaked a tender rose and ultramarine, throwing the ruins into black relief. The village sprawled at the foot of the hill, quiet except for the milk float purring its way along, stopping at each house and rattling bottles. It stopped at the pub, and the tiny, distant figure of the milkman humped two crates of milk to the side door.

Of course, they'd need a lot of milk today—all their letting rooms were occupied by the wedding guests who couldn't be accommodated in the farmhouse, and had stayed overnight. Holly smiled. Mum and Dad really had gone to town, no expense spared so that their youngest daughter would have a day to remember.

Jan and her husband were there, and Mrs Kelly who had come up with Ben and his best man yesterday. And the famous wedding cake had travelled with them, carefully stacked in several graduated boxes beside Mrs K who wouldn't let it out of her sight.

Ben too was staying at the pub, to please Granny, together with Tony Wadebridge, because according to Granny, it was bad luck and improper for the bride and groom to sleep under the same roof on the night before the wedding.

Holly, who had a great rapport with her granny, and knew she was unshockable, was sure that she had made this up, though couldn't figure out why. 'I've heard of not seeing each other on the morning of the wedding,' she'd said, 'but not this.'

'Old Shropshire saying,' Granny had said, making the most of her own particular accent, a mixture of West Country burr and lilting Welsh.

The side door opened as the milkman plonked down the crates and another minuscule figure, blurred by distance, appeared.

'Ben,' breathed Holly.

Just seeing him at a distance made her heart race like the clappers. She splashed her face with cold water and zipped a comb through her hair, rushed down the stairs and out across the dewy lawn and over the field that bordered the long drive. Her ancient striped nightshirt flapped just above her knees and the long wet grass in the field whipped her calves.

They arrived at the foot of the drive together and she hurled herself into his arms. Unsurprised, Ben lifted her off the ground and whirled her round.

'Like the nightie,' he said, rolling his eyes. 'A real turn-on. Is that what you're wearing tonight?'

Holly thought of the minuscule scrap of lace and satin

taking up no room at all in her suitcase. 'That's for me to know and you to find out,' she whispered.

'Oh, I will,' he whispered back, his lips brushing hers. 'It'll be magic, alone together for the first time with hours and days to make love…'

'No pager…'

'No emergencies, no Beth, nor James for a couple of weeks, I love them dearly, but… I long for there to be just the two of us—Dr and Mrs Harvey and all the time in the world, with the future stretching out in front of us. I don't want to be greedy, but just for two magical weeks. I don't want to share you with anyone.' He cupped her face in his hands, his thumbs tenderly stroking her cheek-bones, and gave her a long, lingering kiss of great gentleness, of great promise.

Time passed. He raised his head. His sparkling, dancing, green-hazel eyes were brimful with love.

'Your beautiful morning face,' he said in a hushed voice, scattering butterfly kisses all over it. 'Now go and make yourself even more beautiful for me… See you in church—Mrs Harvey to be.'

He turned and walked away back towards the pub.

Holly watched him go and thought about the kiss, savoured it. She could still feel the gentle pressure of it on her lips. It was like no other kiss that she had ever received. She shivered in the warm, early morning sunshine—it had been a cherishing kiss, a kiss that not only promised a lifetime of loving, but a lifetime of caring too.

Whatever the future brings, she thought, I will remember this kiss all my life.

Holly stood in the porch with her hand in the crook of her father's arm, whilst her bridesmaids were being marshalled into place behind her. She could see into the body of the church. It was crowded with people she had known since she was a child—some villages were still like that, even in the twenty-first century and Abbeyfield was one of them.

But there was a large contingent too of more recent friends, notably those from Lizzie's. They were *en bloc* a few pews back from the front, easy to identify by Sister Birdy's red straw hat with a peacock feather bobbing on top. Beside her, her elfin face beaming, was Carol.

A warm feeling washed over Holly. She trembled slightly, and her bouquet of syringa and roses and honeysuckle shook and shed their delicate perfume.

'You all right, love?' asked her father.

'I'm fine, Dad, absolutely fine,' she replied, her smile radiant.

The bridesmaids were in place, the wedding march rang out—as one, the congregation rose to it's feet.

The Church of the Assumption, Abbeyfield, was large for a village church, and the aisle was a long one. Holly smiled to left and right, but as she got near the altar her eyes became fixed on Ben, splendid in grey morning dress, tailored coat taut across his shoulders. His chestnut hair was bronzed by a sliver of sunlight shafting through a narrow window as he turned to watch her coming towards him.

He put out his hand and took hers as she drew near. Love you, his eyes told her. She handed her bouquet to Amy and gave Ben one of her dazzling, dimpling smiles…

'We are gathered here together…'

'Where are they going for their honeymoon?' people were asking, streaming out of the marquee to see them off.

'No idea,' those asked replied.

'I bet it's somewhere exotic, tropical, expensive, if I know Ben,' said someone.

Granny smiled a secret smile and fingered the paper that Holly had given her. 'Only to be used in extreme emergency,' she had said.

'Mum's the word,' Granny had replied.

Confetti was thrown, rice was thrown. Tin cans, old shoes and unidentifiable objects had been tied to the Range Rover that was to take them on the first leg of their journey.

Hand in hand, they walked along the sandy shore in a mixture of pale daylight and moonlight. The sun had barely dipped below the horizon, in a few hours it would be rising again.

'Granny said that on Skye in high summer, you get two days for the price of one,' said Holly.

'Your granny' murmured Ben, swinging Holly round to face him and pulling her close till their bodies melted into each other, 'is a clever old witch of a woman.'

'A good witch,' whispered Holly, nibbling his ear.

'Oh, undoubtedly a good witch.' Ben pulled her down onto the still warm sand, his body covering hers, his mouth hovering above hers. 'Ever been made love to on a beach in the moonlight?' he asked huskily.

'Never!'

'Nor I. Let's give it a whirl.'

'Why not?' Holly pulled his head down till their lips met. 'I do love you…' her voice was muffled. '…both of you, the old Ben and the new.'

'Love you, too,' said Ben, and started the long, slow, pleasurable business of proving it.

READER SERVICE™

The best romantic fiction direct to your door

Our guarantee to you...

The Reader Service involves you in no obligation to purchase, and is truly a service to you!

There are many extra benefits including a free monthly Newsletter with author interviews, book previews and much more.

Your books are sent direct to your door on 14 days no obligation home approval.

We offer huge discounts on selected books exclusively for subscribers.

Plus, we have a dedicated Customer Care team on hand to answer all your queries on
(UK) 020 8288 2888
(Ireland) 01 278 2062.

GEN/GU/1

MILLS & BOON®

Makes any time special

Copyright © Harlequin Enterprises Limited 1997
All rights reserved

Enjoy a romantic novel from
Mills & Boon®

Presents...™   *Enchanted*™   TEMPTATION®

Historical Romance™   ⊣√ **MEDICAL ROMANCE**

MAT1

⅃MEDICAL ROMANCE™

Fast-paced medical drama

Heart-warming, tender romance

Impossible to put down!

Four new titles available every month

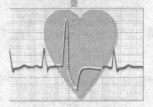

Available from
READER SERVICE™

The best romantic fiction direct to your door

on subscription

GEN/03/RS

For the incurable romantic

MILLS & BOON®

Makes any time special™

Enchanted™

Warm and emotionally fulfilling novels that let you experience the magic of falling in love.

Six brand new titles each month.

Available from the

READER SERVICE™

The best romantic fiction direct to your door

on subscription

GEN/02/RS

MILLS & BOON®

Makes any time special™

*Experience the glamour
and sophistication of*

Presents...™

*Passionate, provocative
romances you'll never want
to end.*

Eight brand new titles each month

Available from the

READER SERVICE™
The best romantic fiction direct to your door

on subscription

GEN/01/RS

Historical Romance™

From Medieval pageantry
to the Restoration
and glittering Regency Seasons

1066 - 1920
all the ages of romance

Four new titles available every month

Available from

READER SERVICE™
The best romantic fiction direct to your door
on subscription

GEN/04/RS

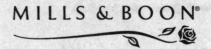

MILLS & BOON®

Fun...

Sensual...

Exciting stories

Four new titles available every month

Available from the

READER SERVICE™

on subscription